PAST ALL HORIZONS

TRAVELER'S TALES: OMNIBUS 1

LEAH R CUTTER

Past All Horizons
Traveler's Tales: Omnibus One
Copyright © 2019 Leah Cutter
All rights reserved
Published by Knotted Road Press
www.KnottedRoadPress.com

The Glass Girl originally published in *Fiction River: Editor's Choice*
Gracie's Fire originally published in *Clockwork Universe: Steampunk Vs. Aliens*
The Curious Case of Rabbit and the Temple Goddess originally published in *Alfred Hitchcock Mystery Magazine*
Sisters originally published in *Fiction River: Unnatural Worlds*

ISBN: 978-1-64470-099-0

Cover and interior design copyright © 2019 Knotted Road Press
http://www.KnottedRoadPress.com

Come someplace new…
Are you a traveler? Do you enjoy exploring strange new worlds, new cultures, new people?

Journey into the various lands envisioned by Leah Cutter.

Sign up for my newsletter and I'll start you on your travels with a free copy of my book, *The Island Sampler*.

I will never spam you or use your email for nefarious purposes. You can also unsubscribe at any time.

http://www.LeahCutter.com/newsletter/

ALSO BY LEAH R CUTTER

The Witch's Progress

Circle of Air

Circle of Water

Circle of Fire

Circle of Earth

Seattle Trolls

The Changeling Troll

The Princess Troll

The Fairy-Bridge Troll

The Troll-Demon War

The Troll-Human War

The Troll-Troll War

The Cassie Stories

Poisoned Pearls

Tainted Waters

Spoiled Harvest

Bloodied Ice

Tanish Empire Trilogy

The Glass Magician

The Desert Heart

The Ghost Dog

INTRODUCTION

Like many writers, I write all over the map.

Seriously. I finally had to go ahead and actually draw out a map so I could give readers a hint about all the different places I was going to take them to.

It hasn't gotten any better as I've gotten older. In fact, it might be worse now, because I have so many novels, and so many combinations of genres that I write in.

I rarely write straight down the center of a single genre. I either mash them up, or as my husband likes to say, it's a genre *plus* something more.

For example, the Shadow Wars trilogy. It's urban fantasy, plus historic fantasy!

I chose the stories for this collection in part to show that variety. There's a bit of everything here: Mystery, superhero, epic fantasy, straight historic, science fiction, steampunk/weird west, horror, and urban fantasy.

While I really do adore most of what I write, I also chose some of my favorite stories for this collection. A lot of these stories have been published other places, so I'm not the only one who really likes them.

Quite a few of these stories are dark, but I also included some very light and silly pieces to balance things out a little. Again, I wanted to take you on a journey, not just to the tops of the mountains but also down through the valleys and into those dark caves just beyond the glen where darker creatures live…

After each story, I've included some notes about either why the story is in this collection, or the circumstances I wrote it under. Some of the stories are inspiration for novels. Some of the stories are the first of several about that particular character. Others are stand alone.

I hope you enjoy this collection, this taste, this journey.

Leah R Cutter
Ravensdale, WA 2019

HELL BY ANY
OTHER NAME

I woke up from my nightmare sitting straight up in bed.

If I could sweat, I'd be drenched. If I had a heart, it would have been beating hard in my chest. If I could breathe, I would have been gasping.

I'd been dreaming of Hell, of course.

Most ghosts, if they admit to sleeping, dream of Hell. It was why we were ghosts. That door to the Beyond wasn't full of pearly gates and choirs of angels. No, it was fire, heat, and chaos.

There were a few ghosts who stayed on Earth even though they were promised Heaven. They were all nuts.

I pressed my hands against my eyes, as if I could shut the images out and wipe them away. No luck. I groaned. Quietly. I didn't want any more complaints from Mrs. H — downstairs about unearthly noises.

I was lucky enough to be able to rent a place outside Ghosttown, to live among the living. Even if it was little more than a glorified closet, with only a skinny, single bed and two stacks of crates holding a door across them that served as my desk. Dark water stains marred the formerly white walls, while mysterious lines crossed the ceiling, shadows of discontent.

The only bright spot was Betsy, my camera, sitting in her corner of the desk. Most of what a ghost sees is muted, grayed, behind the veil still. Betsy always appeared red and glowing, as if a warm heart beat behind her dark lens.

That was all my room contained—one of the advantages of being a ghost. No need to cook or use a bathroom. You couldn't really change your appearance, and since you didn't actually have a body, well, nothing in, nothing out. We still needed rest, though. The brain needed time off to process.

I looked at the clock. Two in the afternoon. I caught

myself before I groaned again. Flames of Hell still licked behind my eyes if I closed them. There would be no more sleep for me that day, though I didn't usually rise until sunset.

I slid aside the heavy drape covering the window, exposing an inch of daylight. I was in luck. Another rainy Seattle day greeted me. I decided to go to Volunteer Park. Might even go to Lakewood Cemetery. Not because I wanted to greet the newly dead; there was a committee for that. Or even to look at the portals, to see if they'd changed. I didn't believe those myths, that I might somehow do enough good that I'd earn Heaven.

No, it was merely a matter of wanting some company of my own kind. I hated to admit it, but sometimes I got lonely. I rose and walked out into the gray haze of the day, the rain sliding through me as if I wasn't really there.

I tried to think of it as a cleansing, inside and out, but I never really feel *clean*.

December 21, 2012 hadn't been the end of the world, only the Great Unraveling. The veils between the Seen and Unseen worlds shredded.

The living suddenly discovered they weren't alone.

Luckily for our side, we had a lot of lawyers. The Interspecies Act passed relatively quickly for Congress, guaranteeing the rights of the dead and others.

Of course, law and practice were often worlds apart. Seattle had one of the stronger lobbies, though. I praised their work again as I got on the bus, the new card system beeping when I passed my hand over it, automatically deducting my fare. I'd hated walking everywhere before.

The bus was mostly empty. A homeless man slumped on a seat next to the back door, arms wrapped firmly around his pack; two students sat next to each other madly texting, probably to each other; and a professionally dressed man with round glasses and a briefcase on his lap sat stiffly in his seat. He stared straight ahead, his face frozen.

As if he'd seen a ghost.

I almost sat next to him, but I'm not generally that vengeful. It's part of what ghosts do, though: scare the living, whether we mean to or not. The ghosts who get off on it were also the ones who, as kids, pulled the wings off flies, and as adults fired people for a living, know what I mean?

Instead, I swayed as the bus turned another corner, making my way to the very last seats in the back, looking out the window and watching the gray day slide by. I could have gone out in the sunshine. Sometimes I enjoyed seeing the world brightly lit, even though it didn't seem as vivid as when I'd been alive. I missed the feeling of warmth, though. And intense sunlight made ghosts less substantial. People no longer saw me. Instead of trying to avoid me, they stepped *through* me. There was no feeling more wrenching than your former intestines momentarily misplaced.

The man with the briefcase got off at the same stop I did. I didn't think anything of it, since he walked straight ahead when I turned left, into the park. I walked up the winding hill, sticking to the sidewalk, not wanting to take a chance on slipping on the wet grass. Red, orange and yellow leaves lay scattered across the green lawn. I remembered, when I was still alive, how colorful the fall leaves were, how a gray day made them seem more vivid.

Dying cast a fog on everything. Nothing was as clear as it used to be. The edges weren't as crisp; the colors, more muted.

I looked through the black donut sculpture at downtown and the Space Needle, and then walked around the reservoir—I'd been alive when it had still been full of water, one of the last open reservoirs in all of Washington. Now it was just a thin pond full of fat koi, algae and bird droppings. Finally, I decided to head north to the cemetery. Walking along the avenue of beechnut trees I saw the man from the bus again. This time he stared straight at me. The hand holding his briefcase was clenched tightly, almost white. With a determined stride, he drew closer. "Andrew Collin?"

"How do you know my name?"

"I need your help."

My mouth must have been gaping because I closed it with a snap. "I only work during business hours," I told him sharply.

"But—"

"If you know my name you already know the address of my office."

I turned on my heel and deliberately walked *through* the nearest tree.

Of course, I appeared on the far side of it. While it was unpleasant for me, I've been told it was distinctly unsettling for the living.

I walked without pause to the cemetery. Only paid professionals among the living ever went there anymore. New memorial parks had sprung up, where the living could go to honor their dead. As a result, cemeteries were one of the safest places on earth. I'd heard stories of more than one attempted robbery or rape ending when the victim fled to a graveyard.

Ghosts could be very vengeful.

Most people avoided graveyards, though, because of the portals, the doors to Heaven or Hell that surround the places of the dead.

The living saw them differently, as shadows, or else they felt them when they walked too close, a chill that went through bones and into the soul. The doors weren't meant for them. Some got glimpses, though, of their afterlife, whether it was angels or seventy-eight virgins or a blessed nothing. The living couldn't pass through. Whatever they saw was disturbing enough they rarely ventured near.

One of the good things about the portals showing up was that all the mass graves were suddenly findable, even in the middle of the jungle. Murderers now had to be very careful where they stashed a body. Portals stuck around even after a soul went through.

Like all ghosts, I found myself drawn to them frequently. We were *meant* to go through. But some could ignore the siren's call better than others.

Flamed licked out of the nearest portal, drawing my attention. A black, churning cloud boiled beyond the burning edges. The only time I felt heat was near that fire. There wasn't a smell of sulfur, or cries of the damned. Just fire I knew would burn my ectoplasmic flesh, and a chasm that would chew up my soul until there was nothing left.

In an abstract manner I admired the contrast between the comforting trees of the park, the dramatic gray of the clouds, and the shooting flames dancing in the portal. I took another step forward, then another, fascinated against my will.

Maybe if I stared long enough, a pattern would form. Maybe I could find a path through the darkness into the light.

Maybe if I wished hard enough, I, too, could grow wings and fly.

I stopped myself in time, before I stepped through, as I always did.

That Hell was not for me.

I wasn't surprised when the guy with the briefcase sat waiting for me in my tiny office in Ghosttown. The door was unlocked, and the living couldn't or wouldn't touch most of the artifacts in the room.

Still, I looked around carefully to make sure nothing had been disturbed. Papers and notebooks, Fixed so that both the living and the dead could touch them, sat stacked in neat piles on the rickety desk. The beat-up file cabinet in the corner, which I kept not only locked but charmed, stood untouched.

Natural artifacts that I'd found—rocks, keys, broken rings, dried flowers, and other knick-knacks—covered the shelves of the cinder block-and-board bookcase that ran along the one wall, exactly in the same pattern as I'd left them. Each of them held a spark of *something*: life, Heaven, energy, I didn't know. All ghosts collected these things. Some Fixers, those among the living with one foot in the world of the dead, used natural artifacts to create other artifacts, electronics and other useful manufactured items dragged far enough out of the Seen world that ghosts could use them, like Betsy, my camera. Other Fixers said it was a lot of hooey.

Me, I just felt better with the natural artifacts surrounding me.

The guy sat stiffly in the guest chair next to the desk. I had to walk past him to get to my own large captain's chair. I made sure to walk by closely, so he could feel the chill that all ghosts emanate.

"What can I help you with, Mr...."

"Potter," he provided. "Harry Potter."

"You're joking, right?"

"My parents were—whimsical."

Though Mr. Potter wore round glasses similar to his namesake, that was where the likeness ended. He looked more like a Danish architect, with perfect blond hair, starched shirt, classic thin blue tie, and charcoal suit.

"So what can I do for you, Mr. Potter?" I picked up the cracked glass fountain pen I kept on the desk and twirled it in my fingers. I'd been a smoker as a young man, and though the ability had disappeared when I'd died, the cravings hadn't.

"Have you heard of Disruption stones?"

"Of course." Every ghost had. Supposedly, they were strong enough to disrupt your fate: if you threw one into a portal, it would change from an image of Hell to Heaven.

"Mine was stolen. I want you to get it back," Mr. Potter said primly.

I couldn't help it. I had to laugh. "First off, why would I believe you? They're just myths. Next, even if I did believe you, why would you come to a ghost to retrieve it? Why wouldn't I just take it for myself?"

"Most of the myths about them aren't true," Mr. Potter explained. His voice took on a lecturing tone. "They're manufactured, not found or mined. They must be Fixed to an individual, like an artifact. They're horribly expensive, both in time and materials. Like an artifact, only a ghost can touch one. However, only the ghost of the person it's been made for can use it."

"So, someone stole something useless from you," I stated, still not believing him.

For the first time, Mr. Potter showed a streak of anger. "More myths," he said darkly. "Some people erroneously believe they can re-Fix a stone. That a strong enough Fixer can realign it. They're wrong, of course. The thief will destroy it by attempting to change the Fixing."

"Mr. Potter, I investigate missing people, or cheating husbands or wives. I collect evidence for the court. I don't specialize in artifacts. There are others who do. Let me recommend—"

"I don't want *them*. I want you. I investigated you. Thoroughly."

"Really," I said in my driest voice. I had practiced the tone, working to keep out the ghostly overtones.

Mr. Potter paled only slightly, so I thought I'd mostly succeeded.

"You were a cop—"

"Detective," I growled.

Mr. Potter swallowed, then continued. "Detective. With an impressive close rate."

"Not all of those cases were closed cleanly." The Interspecies Act had ensured that the dead weren't necessarily prosecuted for crimes committed while living.

Lots of lawyers on our side.

"You also go that extra mile now," Mr. Potter added. "A very satisfied client list."

"A confidential list of clients," I said, glancing again at my locked file cabinet. Two weeks prior I had noticed something off when I'd come in, as if the locking spell had started to slide. I'd assumed at the time that the spell for shocking anything that physically touched the metal had worn off and I just needed the building Witch to reapply it.

I couldn't be paranoid enough, it seemed.

"People talk," Mr. Potter said with a fake smile. "Particularly with the right monetary incentive."

I bristled. "And you think that will work with me?"

"Triple your normal fee? Yes, I do."

"I won't be bought." Criminals had discovered that early, and I'd carried the habit into the afterlife.

"I'm not asking you to do anything wrong or illegal. Merely to retrieve an artifact that's mine and has been stolen from me."

"Why should I take your word that it's yours?"

"Here's the name of the ghost who stole it," Mr. Potter said. "And the man who paid her." He slid a piece of paper across the desk.

I recognized only the first name. Toni Hermino. Beautiful Italian immigrant. She'd been a thief when she'd been alive, specializing in exotic gems and jewelry. Now that she'd passed over, she focused on artifacts and art.

"Go talk with her. Verify my story. Check me out as well. As an extra incentive, when you return the stone, I'll share the list of ingredients needed to make a Disruption stone for yourself."

I scoffed. "Just the cash is fine."

I didn't believe in this mythical stone. Mr. Potter did. He was seemed to be an intelligent businessman, not given to flights of fancy. Either someone had snowed him good, or there was actually something to this myth.

"I'll pay Toni a visit," I said grudgingly. "But that's all I'm agreeing to do for now."

"Wonderful," Mr. Potter said, his smile full of teeth.

Fortunately for me, he wasn't the only one with a bite.

The Haunting Hour art gallery didn't open until midnight, of course. I spent the time at one of the Fixed terminals in the library, cruising the electronic highway that ran easily through the Seen and Unseen worlds, investigating Mr. Potter and his nemesis. The three other terminals were empty, their screens glowing with that odd half-light of the almost there. Though the living still manned the desks, mostly ghosts wandered between the stacks, seeking treasures they'd missed in their youth, answers for their unending existence.

Mr. Potter, I learned, worked as a long-term investment banker for the dead. Believe me, there was no one more committed to long term than a ghost with no fear of dying. He'd done well for himself—nice Craftsman on Queen Anne Hill, second cottage out on the San Juan Islands. Divorced, no kids, mother in a very expensive, private nursing home. No charges, no official investigations, not even a letter of complaint.

Squeaky clean.

Something about him still set my ectoplasm crawling.

I arrived at the gallery soon after it opened. The long windows cast brilliant light out onto the dark street. More people than I'd expected clomped across its hardwood floors: some sort of open house. The living walked in groups of two or three, clutching wine glasses and making hushed commentary.

I wouldn't call the images on the walls "art." The drive to create such things, that passion, belonged solely with the living. This was a façade. To me, every piece looked the same, like chalkboards badly cleaned, with squiggling green, glowing lines drifting across them. As a line crossed a boundary of a piece, it turned into smoke and dissipated.

There were very few ghosts who were once artists: no matter their destination, anything was better than a pale existence.

Toni chatted with two guests, accepting their studied praise for the show and the artist. I waited patiently as Toni drew pledges of donations from them for a dubious charity.

I didn't say anything or try to warn them away. I wasn't a detective anymore, and as ghost, it was hard to make a living.

"So, *paisano*, what can I do for you this wicked evening?" Toni smiled like she meant it. She'd probably been stunning when she'd been alive. Now, she was as pale as all of us, her beautiful dress just a shade different than her skin, still clinging to nice curves and shapely calves accentuated with high heels.

"Just checking on a rumor," I told her. "A myth."

"Myth? You? I thought *polizia* were only concerned with facts. "

I didn't bother to correct her assumption. Once a cop, always a cop. "Sometimes disproving something is as important," I said smoothly.

Toni cocked an eyebrow at me.

Maybe not that smooth.

"I've heard...rumors that maybe a precious stone was removed from a magician's house. Care to comment?"

"Ah. If, perhaps, I knew of the possibility of such a thing, how would you show your appreciation?"

I pressed my lips together and rocked back on my heels. I'd expected Toni to deny everything.

It meant she wanted to tell me something.

A too-human laugh interrupted my thoughts. We both looked at the source then looked away.

The dead rarely laughed.

"A favor," I said, rolling the dice. "Big or small. Some future claim."

"Interesting," Toni said, but she was already nodding. "Yes. A future favor it is."

Toni grew pensive and stepped forward, her voice a hitching whisper. I easily caught it, whereas anyone living would draw away from the sibilant, haunting tones.

"A precious stone, such as what you're asking about, if it exists, would be cold, so cold. A little piece, like that," she said, holding up her fingers and indicating a mere inch. "Very heavy." Her eyes took on a distant look. "It was—it would not—be right. Not natural. Not good."

Toni glanced up at me out of the corner of her eye. "Removing such a thing from its owner might not be bad, no?" She ended with a shrug.

I shrugged back. "Depends on who got it next. What they plan to do with it."

At that, Toni smiled. "Such a person might be very arrogant. They might think they can change the nature of the thing. They'll just destroy it. No harm done."

"What if someone was hired to bring the stone back to the magician?"

"I would call him a fool," Toni said coldly.

When I said nothing, Toni nodded her head once, sharply. "I have guests waiting," she told me, looking away.

"Thank you." I turned and headed toward the door, ignoring the whispering humans.

"The magician's castle—" Toni called from behind me.

I paused.

"It's more dangerous than the rest."

When nothing else seemed to be forth-coming, I nodded my thanks and left, walking out of the brightly lit gallery and into the dark of the street. Of course the night didn't hide me—no, here I was more visible. I had my own glow, like all ghosts after midnight.

I wished I could change my clothes, somehow. Pull up my collar. Tug on my sleeves. Something to give myself a sense of protection.

I didn't want to go through with this job. Mr. Potter was a snake. I knew I should walk away before he stuck his fangs in me.

However, I couldn't shake the feeling that something else was going on. A bigger game.

This part of the magician's story had checked out. Now it was time to go see the arrogant man.

Mr. A—, short for arrogant, as Toni had so aptly named him, lived only a few blocks away from Mr. Potter, even higher on Queen Anne Hill. A quaint, brick wall separated the yard from the sidewalk, while the yard's sloping incline separated the house from its neighbors, giving it the impression of a feudal castle snubbing those beneath it. It was done in pseudo-Tudor style, with wide, dark planks separating the white stucco. More than one gable peered darkly over the expanse, sticking out from the steeply slanted roof.

The garden was immaculate, of course, the hedges trimmed with tweezers and the grass probably not merely cut, but each blade filed to a precise angle.

Ghosts generally hung out in one or two places in a house like Mr. A—'s: up in the attic, snuggled into the rafters and listening to the rain, or deep in the cellars.

I'd brought Betsy with me on this trip. Generally, I used her only for photographing cheating husbands or stealthy wives, but Betsy had other talents as well.

The Fixer I'd used for Betsy had been new to the business. She'd had to try more than once to bring Betsy "over" so that I could use the camera. The Fixer had spent a lot of energy, and hadn't charged me much money, because neither of us had realized what she'd done until much later.

She'd made Betsy into a spectralgraph.

As easily as I took pictures of humans, I could also take pictures of things such as houses or cars—anything manufactured—and see any residual spectral effect.

I took pictures of the houses next to Mr. A—'s first. I needed to make sure there wasn't any environmental influence. I seemed to be in luck. This part of the hill hadn't been declared holy, nor did it contain an ancient burial mound. If it had, every house in the vicinity would have a low-level spectral reading.

Then I took a picture of Mr. A—'s place.

It was lit up like the Castro District on Halloween.

Which meant either it was ghost central, or it housed not just a few, but an entire museum's worth of powerful artifacts. As I hadn't seen another ghost anywhere on the street, I had to assume the latter.

Caution told me to wait until broad daylight, when I could approach the house unseen, hidden by the sun.

I told caution where to stick it and climbed the stairs up to the house. That was when I had my first big shock.

The house was *Sealed*.

Not just the doors and windows locked, no. Every bit of folklore, both the things that did and didn't work, were employed around the perimeter. A band of salt, at least half a foot wide, had been drawn in a circle around the property. Rowan branches rested on every windowsill. Ba Gua mirrors hung over the door. Bottle trees flush with blessings and curses were planted every few feet.

Why the Hell hadn't Toni warned me about *this* place?

I slowly circled the house, counter clockwise, seeking a crack in its protection.

Nada.

In the back, where the neighbors couldn't see, additional protections had been laid: a sticky rope web that had been Fixed. Dancing spectral lights guaranteed to confuse the more weak-willed. Running water from a fountain rolled past half the house like an old fashioned moat.

I had no idea if the house held just as much protection against the living as well. I had to assume it did. I also had to assume that the security cameras mounted every few feet had also been Fixed and were now tracking me.

I had to get out of there before they released their equivalent of Hell hounds.

The moat drew me back. The flowing water had to come from somewhere; a pump, deep inside. It wasn't a naturally flowing spring. Down, underground, it was being recycled. The circle would be broken there.

A light came on, shining out a second story window above me.

Without thinking, I sank *down*, into the ground.

Scientists who have studied the phenomenon have reported that ghosts take on different shapes underground. Some become snakelike; others, more of an amorphous blob.

Me, I've always felt as though I grew round, with a hard skin, like a ping-pong ball. I didn't lose myself or any consciousness, but I know I was very different underground than above it.

Black dirt slid easily around my compact form. Roots parted before me like a tangled curtain. An earthworm blindly kept pace with me as I burrowed through the rich loam.

I couldn't see anything—at least, not in a human sense, with eyes. I was as sightless as the worm. But I sensed that sliver of a crack before me, like a door just barely ajar, its light spilling out into the darkness. It drew me like the sun draws a seedling, that single bright spot in the unending night.

Coldness bracketed me as I eased inside, my natural form tumbling into shape. I stood, stretched, imagining my vertebrae cracking in relief, though I didn't feel anything, actually. I almost groaned, but stopped myself just in time.

The room I'd landed in had piles of boxes against the walls. One of the bottom ones had broken open, crushed by the weight of the boxes on top of it. Its spilled contents had disturbed the delicate chalk lines drawn across the floor, a gypsy sigil to keep out the undead.

I skirted the edges of the drawing, pressed up next to the boxes. Whoever had drawn this had known what they were doing. When I reached the door, I snapped a couple of pictures of it with Betsy. Someone, somewhere, probably knew how to break this one from our side.

The hall I stepped into was as plain as the room I'd just come from. It had been recently painted, with a yellowed linoleum floor and doorways lining the walls. If I'd been thorough, I would have looked in each room, taken pictures of the spells I was sure I'd find there.

But the room at the end hummed with power. I didn't need Betsy's eye to tell me powerful artifacts lay behind it.

Ghosts looked the same, felt the same, every damn day of their existence.

As I drew closer to this room, the hairs on the back of my neck rose up. An actual shiver went down my spine.

It was too seductive for words.

I walked straight through the door into the room without another thought.

Of course, a sigil lay just on the other side. I'd blundered right into it. Caught like an ant in amber, I couldn't move, couldn't sink into the ground or mist away. I was held right there until someone came and freed me.

I tried to compose myself. A security camera had turned deliberately toward me and held me in its sight. Might as well see what was here. Shelves held row after row of artifacts and Fixed items. I didn't recognize any of them, just felt their power. I looked for a stone, anything that might have felt "heavy" or "cold," but nothing struck me that way. Or rather, no stone did. There was a doll's hand that felt "off" to me, and some brown, curled leaves that shifted as if unseen bugs crawled over and under them.

I ignored the first twinge I felt in the center of my back. I was still too busy gawking like some damn tourist.

The second one came with the wonderment of pain.

How was that happening to me? I looked down at the lines drawn in raised chalk. The design appeared to be a standard Chinese holding spell.

Another pain wracked me, this time starting in my gut.

Only then did I really notice the second artifact that had swung in my direction when I'd stumbled in. At first I mistook it for a camera, but no, it was actually some kind of gun.

Like the Disruption stones, rumors of these sorts of things had been around forever, some sort of technology that could be used to banish a ghost.

I struggled wildly then, trying to get free. I'd been banished before. It wasn't fun.

This time it wasn't the abrupt pain of being shoved from the world. No. This was a pulling, like being quartered with Clydesdales, slowly but inevitably tearing each limb off and away.

I bellowed, shrieked, and moaned, causing the very foundation of the house to shake, but to no avail.

I was torn asunder.

I became corporeal—or at least, a ghost again—in the graveyard where my bones lay buried.

Betsy, of course, was gone.

All the portals sprang up, showing images of flame and chaos as I rose. I ignored them and the false comfort of light they provided in the darkness. They looked less out of place than the sign for the cemetery itself. Who puts a flashing neon time-and-date sign at the entrance of a graveyard?

Buses had long stopped running, and no cab would ever pick up a ghost. I started the long walk back downtown. I longed for a cigarette, anything to break the monotony of walking. Though I could move more quickly than the living, it was still going to take a damn long time.

I thought about my options as I trudged back to the city.

Go back to Mr. A—'s and retrieve Betsy. Not practical. Probably not possible. But I'd miss her. She'd been my only touchstone in this existence.

Find Mr. Potter and tell him I'd failed. Then I'd be out my fee as well as my camera.

I couldn't think how Toni might be able to help. She'd already warned me. I didn't have a thing she wanted, I was certain. And I already owed her a debt. I certainly couldn't pay her to go steal Betsy back for me.

With the sun rising, Hell's bells sounding in the blazing light, I was too tired to think anymore. I went back to my room instead, collapsing on my bed and hoping that something besides nightmares would come in my sleep.

This time I dreamed of being banished and never able to come back, floating amorphous above the graveyard like a lonely cloud.

I can't say it was an improvement over dreaming about Hell.

By midafternoon I finally decided I'd had enough of pretending to sleep. I was still no closer to a plan of action. Mr. A—, of the impenetrable house, still had the Disruption stone, and given the number and strength of the other artifacts he had, I was almost ready to believe that myth.

And now he had Betsy. Her usual seat on my desk looked naked without her. This place was still a dump, barely room to walk, a mere mattress on a rusted iron frame, but it was where I hung my hat, and Betsy made it, if not home, at least mine.

I knew Mr. A— would have either fixed the crack in his defenses or he would have widened it, placing a trap on the other side.

That didn't stop me from going back there when I realized that the clouds had burned away, leaving miles of blue sky and bright light.

After a bus ride of being trampled on and brushed through, I felt exhausted and out of place. I didn't stop my groan when I looked up that steep hill I was going to have to climb. It wouldn't be physically tiring, not as it might have been when I'd been alive. It took will, though, and I'd been pushing myself for a while.

The Puget Sound shone blue beneath the hill, boats and ships, large and small, skimming across it. Wind I couldn't feel swirled the dried leaves on the sidewalk. I couldn't smell the air, but I knew it would be crisp and clean.

The fake Tudor house looked the same as the night before: dark windows, perfect lawn, graceful walk—

—that led to a gaping-open front door.

I told myself it was my former detective instincts kicking in. Mr. A— was far too paranoid to leave his front door open. Something had to be wrong.

Honestly, though, I just wanted a way into that house.

I raced up the path, flowing as fast as the wind, when

Mr. Potter stepped across the threshold. He shook hands with Mr. A—, the pair of them laughing.

I couldn't help my low growl. They appeared to be on very cordial terms.

I pushed myself into bush next to the walk. Twigs rammed through my gut and lungs, branches pinned my arms. Though I didn't need to breath, my lungs felt constricted, as if there weren't enough air. If I could sweat, despite the cool day I would have felt it trickling down my forehead and back. I made myself stand very still, blending into the bush, fading with the light.

Though Mr. Potter wore different glasses that day— white rimmed, very European—they didn't help him see me.

Or he never would have brought Betsy out of his bag.

———————

I waited until full night before I went to beard the magician in his own den. I wanted him to see me this time. I'd wasted away the rest of the afternoon in a park, sitting on an isolated bench facing the trees. No other ghost came by, just a wind that made the living shiver and the trees dance. I had no arguments planned. I just wanted to finish this. Get Betsy and run.

Of course, it wasn't going to be that easy.

The windows of Mr. Potter's house that looked out over the street were leaded in the upper part: old glass that ran with time, looking heavier than it ought to. When I drew near, I figured out why. Mr. Potter's house had protections similar to Mr. A—'s. Someone had drawn lines of protection around every gray shingle on the walls as well as on the lead of the windows. Knotted rope lay against the foundation, salt infused to its core.

I walked around the house, keeping to the stone walkway, not daring to step off it in case there were other traps I didn't see.

The crack in the house's protection was deliberate. The door to the root cellar had been left bare.

No choice but to go in that way. I flowed through the door but didn't step onto the floor. Who knew what kind of sigils had been engraved there?

However, I was overly cautious. The neat tile floor of the laundry room held no chalk, paint, or dried chicken blood. A navy blue washer and dryer sat in one corner and Mr. Potter sat in a chair next to them, reading something on a tablet. "I've been expecting you," he said, putting his reading material down and standing. "I need to pay you the rest of your fee."

"You lied to me," I told Mr. Potter's retreating back.

"Not a big lie. Not really. Toni did steal the stone from me, to help me shore up my defenses. Mr. A— had bet me that no one could beat his, which more than made up the fee I'm paying you."

Only then did Mr. Potter realize I hadn't followed him. I'd seen too many sigils and curses in his buddy's house. I wasn't going to be caught again.

"Don't you trust me?" Mr. Potter said, seemingly aggrieved.

"No, I don't. Now give me Bet—my camera. And never contact me again."

A loud, human groan came from behind the door Mr. Potter had opened. He gave me an odd half-smile. "That might be someone hurt. You should go see."

I stayed where I was. If there was a person in there, I

couldn't do anything for them. I couldn't touch them. Chances were the presence of a ghost wouldn't comfort them, either.

Another groan slithered through the air.

"Damn it. Potter, what are you playing at?"

"Come see," he said, beckoning.

I should have left. Hell, I should have *run* as quickly and as far away as I could.

The third groan ended with a pained whimper.

Obviously, I had more humanity left in me than Mr. Potter because I flowed into the room.

A skinny, bearded man lay on a long table pushed against the far wall. His clothes were mismatched and filthy; he was probably homeless. He'd been stabbed in the gut. Blood pooled over the hands he had clenched to his abdomen. From my years on the force I knew it was already too late. He was bleeding out.

The door behind me slammed shut. Of course, the room was *Sealed*. Not a single crack that I could escape through.

"Hey, buddy," I said to the homeless man. His eyes were glazed over and he couldn't see me. Couldn't hear me. I reached out my hand, but I knew if I tried to touch him with it, it would just sink through him.

"What now, Potter?" I asked, looking around. A single window sat high above me, with an ancient shoot underneath it. This used to be the coal room, I realized. More recently, it had held the firewood for the house. Split logs lay in neat piles across the other wall. A handy ax leaned against them.

I couldn't touch or manipulate anything in the room.

"Now, you leave." Mr. Potter's voice came in clear over hidden speakers.

"Afraid you're going to have to open the door," I told him. The floor was cement, but had been reinforced with lead and was impossible to sink into.

"I don't have to. He will."

The homeless man coughed once, a death rattle. Hollywood has tried to emulate that sound for decades, but they'd never come close to the real thing. It was enough to give a ghost chills.

"Your kind is wrong," Mr. Potter continued. "You should all be forced to go Beyond, where you belong."

I hadn't taken Potter for a bigot. He worked for the dead.

No—he worked for their *money*.

"You don't really care about us, ghosts or the dead," I told him. "You just want to keep everything you've stolen from them. That's why your house is so protected, as well as Mr. A—'s. Your pious act is justification for your petty crimes."

Mr. Potter chuckled. "Very astute. However, my crimes are far from petty. You've seen my accounts?"

I had, as well as the contracts that signed everything over to his firm once the dead did pass Beyond. Shaking my head, I replied, "Petty." Ghosts never trusted the living completely. "None of them have given you full access to their resources."

"But the promise of a Disruption stone makes them much more amenable," Mr. Potter said smugly.

I scoffed. "Still a myth."

"No, I have—ah."

The homeless guy on the table had finally died.

I'd never seen a spirit rise before. This, I learned, Hollywood had gotten right. A younger, better-dressed version of the man sat up, pale and, well, ghostly, while his body stayed on the table.

A portal to Heaven sprang up instantly. All bright blue sky and endless green fields—some kind of pastoral afterlife.

Would have bored me to tears. Still. Lucky bastard.

Without even a glance in my direction, he swung his legs down and walked straight through.

As soon as he'd passed, the portal turned black. Flames lined the arch and clouds gathered.

I finally realized I was doomed.

Mr. Potter had laid a clever trap. My only way out of this room was through that. Eventually I'd crack. Potter knew it. I couldn't resist forever, not in a locked room, not with that constant siren's call.

"Let me out, Potter," I told him one last time, unable to tear my eyes from the flames now licking outside the doorway.

"Go back where you belong," Potter hissed.

"See you in Hell," I said.

Then I moaned.

I closed my eyes and put everything into it, giving voice to my unearthly displeasure.

"What are you doing?" Mr. Potter said.

He didn't sound panicked. Not yet.

I moaned, repeatedly, louder and louder, sending waves of sound through the foundation of the house, through the walls, shaking the core of all who heard.

"Stop!" Potter screamed.

I didn't.

Mr. Potter had forgotten that ghosts are creatures of the dead.

Though we prided ourselves on adjusting to modern

life, at our core, we still did one thing best: haunting the living—terrifying them.

Sometimes to death.

A ringing knock on the door finally made me scale back my yowling. I didn't know how long I'd been there, singing the songs of the dead. The flames of the portal danced in time with me, cackling hellfire, pleased, I think, with the terror I'd rained down.

An officer whom I'd met when I'd been alive stuck his head in the door. "Hey, Andy."

"Ed."

He took out his earplugs, then led the way out of the room and upstairs. He spoke as he walked. "Potter ran into the street and directly into an oncoming car. He's at the hospital now. Unconscious. They don't know if he'll regain consciousness." Ed didn't look at me.

I hoped the bastard died while dreaming of my haunting.

"The whole thing is taped here," Ed told me, leading me into Mr. Potter's study and showing me the four large plasma screens on the desk. "We know it was self-defense. You'll still have to come down to the station and give a statement."

"Fine by me." Potter's study didn't hold as many artifacts as I thought it might. The only one I wanted to see was Betsy, and there she was, waiting for me.

Ed didn't say anything as I scooped her up.

He couldn't see the small, heavy rock sitting next to her, or how I picked it up as well.

By the time I finished at the station, late afternoon had come again with familiar clouds and rain. I had the officer drop me off at Volunteer Park and made my way directly back to Lakewood Cemetery. I walked through the wet grass, remembering its former brilliant green. More trees stood bare now—must have been a storm the previous night. I nodded to a few of my fellow ghosts, whispering to each other near a grave, then made my way alone to a bench where I could watch the flickering portals.

The stone weighed heavily in my pocket. Cold, too, like a frozen piece of night.

Or maybe not night, but nightmare.

Pious didn't buy you Heaven. Being a bastard didn't necessarily mean Hell, either. You had to believe in good, as well as do it, was the theory of the day.

Me, I'd been a pessimistic bastard all my life, as well as far into my death.

I don't know why I tried to change my luck. When I walked to the nearest portal it flickered, growing dark. I watched the unending flames, the hungry clouds, then finally tossed the stone inside.

Unlike a real stone, it didn't land on the other side, but stayed somewhere Beyond.

Nothing changed until I turned to go.

Suddenly, sunlight shone through the gateway. My beloved city of Seattle lay stretched out on the other side. My heart ached to be there, to go *home*. Even without stepping through, I knew it would be perfect. I would know everyone I met, and if I didn't, they'd still be friends. There would be good food and wine, endless talk and laughter interspersed with quiet time in the hills and on the water. There would be books and time to read them, music and dance whenever I wanted.

I still walked away.

It wasn't mine. I hadn't earned it. I couldn't be bought. Not then, not now.

I turned back to the gray Seattle day, knowing I'd never win that clean, beautiful city...but that I still had to try.

AUTHOR'S NOTES

Hell By Any Other Name was written as the first short story in a challenge that I set for myself, to write, edit, and publish a short story a week, every week for thirteen weeks. (This later became the *Baker's Dozen* collection.)

I had known I wanted to write a ghost story. I had gone out with someone the night before, and had ended up talking a lot about ghosts. When I woke up the next morning, most of this world was in my head: Andy, the shredded veils, and Betsy.

There are several stories about Andy and the others. I have them all collected together in *The Shredded Veil Mysteries*.

THE GLASS GIRL

URRRRGGGGH! That Daiki thinks he's so special. Just because he's cute and smart and...

Who am I kidding? He is *that special. And me? I'm just this girl.*

Sakura leaned back against her desk chair with a sigh, throwing her pen down on her journal. She didn't have a chance with Daiki. Or Shou. Or any of the other boys.

They were always too involved with their stupid video games and their basketball and their phones. They would never even notice a shy girl like her. She was as mousy as Kaori, one of her favorite anime characters.

At least Kaori was smart. And could win at Mahjong just by glancing at the board. While Sakura had to study and work hard at her grades. There was no magic spirit horse to ride away on, no matter how she might try to transport herself into the posters that covered her walls. No magical cat bus to take her away from the hustle of Tokyo and out into quiet green hills.

Sakura sighed and pushed her journal to the side, reaching for her school books.

Wait. Gross! What was wrong with her hand?

Sakura held up her right hand. It had *changed.* Instead of flesh, it had transformed into glass, along with her wrist and half of her forearm.

Not smooth glass, no. From her knuckles grew sharp ridges down the back of her hand. Other ridges joined them, from her thumb and down her wrist. Only her palm was smooth.

She moved her wrist in circles. Her hand felt the same. And she couldn't see through the glass. An iridescent material lay in strips inside the glass, reflecting back the light in all the colors of the rainbow.

If Sakura peered very closely and held her hand at an

angle, she could see the tiny bones of her wrist. They actually looked smaller than they should be, as if viewed from a great distance.

Cautiously, Sakura stuck her tongue out to taste one of the glass ridges. It was sharp enough that it would cut her if she wasn't careful. But it tasted like nothing—just the feel of a cool, unyielding surface against her tongue.

Her hand didn't feel her tongue, couldn't feel her hot breath when she blew on it. It was like she wore a glass glove.

What was happening to her? And why? There hadn't been any earthquake recently that had released some unnatural gas trapped beneath the earth since the Old Ages, had there? Or some nuclear explosion, or even aliens come to visit? She checked her phone but nothing popped up on the news.

Not that she believed the manga in which she read about such things.

In a gradual wave, Sakura's skin came back. Her hand returned to normal. She could feel everything again.

What had just happened? She'd never read a story about a girl turning into glass, or being turned into glass by an evil sorcerer. She was pretty sure she didn't know an evil sorcerer. Not even Mrs. Tomagatchi who lived in the flat above theirs.

Should she tell her mom? Maybe it was some ancient family curse that was only visited on females every third generation or something. It would be just like her mom not to tell her something important like that.

But how could she prove what had happened? If it wasn't something in the family, her mom wouldn't believe her. And besides, her mom had enough to worry about with her younger brother, Takumi, in the hospital again.

No, Sakura had to actually become glass before she told her mom about it.

Geez, what would happen if she had some kind of transformation at school? That would be just her luck. She could see it now—she'd just gotten up the courage to talk with Daiki and *wham*, she'd be glass instead.

He'd probably just look up from whatever game he was playing and proclaim her gross.

Great. This was just what she needed to have to worry about, in addition to boys and grades and her friends and her brother and everything else. Turning into glass in front of everyone. Showing her...everything, to everyone.

Being a teenager sucked.

Fortunately, no part of Sakura turned into glass again while she was at school, not even during the horrible history test in the afternoon.

Afterward school, Sakura sat on one of the large round cushions in the common area, waiting for her friends. Sun shone through the floor to ceiling windows, making the atrium bright. Groups of students chatted in clusters, boys on one side, girls on the other. Daiki passed by with his friends.

Of course, he didn't notice her sitting there, all alone.

Aiko came up first and plopped down right next to Sakura, practically in her lap.

What was it, couldn't her friends see her either? She still put her arm across her friend's back.

Aiko sighed and leaned her head against Sakura's shoulder. "I hate math," she complained.

Sakura giggled. "And history. And physics. And English studies. And—"

Aiko laughed. "I know. I know. Let's just say that *school* isn't my favorite subject."

Sakura nodded and leaned into her friend.

"I'm glad it was you here first," Aiko said quietly as she slipped her hand into Sakura's.

"Why is that?" Sakura asked, growing alarmed. Did Aiko have some big secret that she only wanted to share with Sakura? Maybe some secret crush?

"Relax," Aiko said, giggling some more. "It's just that you're more comfortable to be around than the others." She shrugged her shoulders and sighed. "You make school less gross."

Before Sakura could reply, Yuuka and Natsuki came up. "Ice cream!" they declared happily.

Aiko immediately leapt to her feet as if she was no longer tired, had never been tired or heart sore. "Count me in!" she exclaimed gladly.

Sakura shouldered her bag and rose. "But only for a little while. Then I have to get home and study."

The other three girls nodded. They also had a large workload that night—every night.

"How's your brother?" Yuuka asked as they walked out of the building and onto the crowded street.

Sakura shrugged. "His white blood cell count hasn't risen. But it hasn't dropped anymore either."

The specter of cancer loomed, of course, but the doctors really didn't know what they were dealing with. As usual, with her brother.

Sakura knew better than to suggest vampire chibis, but it would have explained a lot.

"You okay?" Yuuka asked. "You were quiet today. Well, quieter than normal."

Sakura nodded, surprised and touched that her friends had noticed. "It's just...everything," she decided on.

How could she explain to even her friends that she might be a complete and total freak of nature and sometimes turned into glass?

"I know," Yuuka said. She also took hold of Sakura's hand.

Everyone was getting really touchy. Was Sakura broadcasting that she was in that bad of shape?

Still, she walked hand in hand and arm in arm with her friends to the ice cream shop, ready to fortify herself with red-bean-mocha goodness before going back home.

Sakura's entire arm turned to glass that night while she was studying. Of course, Mom wasn't at home—she was at the hospital. Sakura was on her own that night.

The ridges from Sakura's knuckles continued all the way up her arm. The sleeve of her blouse disappeared at the edge of the glass.

Awesome. So it wasn't as if she would change into glass underneath her clothes. No, her clothes were going to disappear as well.

Though her arm was completely made of glass, it didn't feel fragile to Sakura. The ridges were solid and the edges sharp. Her arm felt completely normal, despite how it looked.

Sakura took a picture of herself and her glass arm in the mirror. However, the photo showed a normal teenaged girl, still in the white shirt of her school uniform, untucked from her black skirt, blue-and-green argyle socks rolled up over her knees, her long black hair held back in a bun wrapped around a pencil.

But her arm looked perfectly normal.

Did this mean she was really going crazy? That no one else could see her turn to glass?

Maybe it wouldn't be completely awful if she transformed during the middle of the day, while she was at school.

She still felt…vulnerable, with her arm all glass. Like anyone could see inside her, see the tiny bones that made up her arm.

But she had another test to study for. And no proof of a curse or magic spell.

Her arm went back to normal fairly quickly, and Sakura returned to studying.

The following two nights, more and more of Sakura turned into glass. It didn't always happen at the same time. Sometimes it happened right after dinner. Other times, just before she was ready to go to bed.

When she fully transformed into glass, Sakura made herself go and stand in front of the tall mirror.

She didn't really look human anymore. Her ridged arms went up to a square chest that dropped down just past her hips. Her legs stuck out from underneath that, like a girl wearing a wooden placket advertising cigarettes or a new mobile game. Her face hadn't changed much. It was the only part of her that remained flesh, placed precariously on top of her boxy glass body.

Her eyes had gone completely gray, though, with no whites or pupil, just a gray cloudiness.

In the center of her deeply ridged chest glowed a warm red light. It was a happy red, comforting. It looked like there was a jewel hanging in the center of her square chest.

What was that for? It looked important.

Sakura peered closer. At least she couldn't see anything private through the glass, like her breasts. The red light obliterated all that.

Sakura checked along her sides. She didn't have any seams that she could find, no way to get at the jewel without tearing her body apart. And she didn't feel comfortable doing that.

The glow and her glass body faded, leaving her a regular teenaged girl, still dressed in her school uniform.

Disappointed, Sakura returned to her desk to do more studying.

She couldn't just be turning into glass for nothing. There had to be some reason, some purpose.

She just had to find it.

The next night, Sakura found herself fully changed again. Unlike the other nights, this time, she felt restless.

She hesitated before opening the door from her tiny room to the rest of the apartment. Did she really want to show her mother? What would she say?

Sakura didn't want to add to her mother's worries. The doctors were talking chemo and other treatments for leukemia for her brother, if only they could get him stabilized.

Yet, Sakura was also curious if her mother could actually see her transformation.

Sakura crept down the hall. The walls were filled with so many pictures, pictures of them all together before Dad had been killed in the car accident, her younger brother Takumi with Sakura at the Sensō-ji temple, holding their *joss* sticks, Grandma and Grandpa toasting saki together.

Mom stood stirring something on the stove. The kitchen smelled of garlic and chicken soup, fresh onions and rice.

"Mom?" Sakura queried, staying where she was in the doorway to the kitchen.

"Hmmm?" Mom said, looking up. "Who is that?" She squinted her eyes. "Oh. Hello dear."

Sakura took a deep breath. Mom *couldn't* see her changed self, see the glass.

That was a good thing, right?

Mom held out an arm. Sakura scooted right over, then hesitated. She didn't want to accidentally cut her mom with her sharp glass ridges.

But Mom didn't seem to notice and slid her arm over Sakura's shoulders as if there weren't ridges there at all.

With a relieved sigh, Sakura snuggled in, wrapping both her arms around her mother's waist, leaning her head against her mother's collarbone.

It was an odd feeling, being glass and holding onto her mom. She couldn't feel like she normally did, didn't feel her mom's warmth or the solidity of her body. It was more like holding onto a braided ribbon that kept twisting in the wind, something frail and shallow.

It scared Sakura to think of her mom as frail. She'd been their rock after Dad had died.

Plus, Sakura had to bend more than she used to, in order to place her head on her mom's collarbone.

She was growing again. She'd be taller than her mom one day. She suppressed her shivers as a good daughter should.

Mom kissed Sakura's head. "I'm glad you came out," Mom said, "instead of hiding in your room all night again."

Sakura shrugged. "I've been…busy," she said.

Since her mom couldn't see that she'd turned into glass, Sakura wasn't about to bring it up.

"It's just that seeing you reminded me of the good things that we still have," Mom said softly. "I know, you think I'm a sentimental old fool. But you give me hope."

Long after Sakura went to bed she kept thinking about her mom's statement.

Her friends at school had all started to touch her more often. Aiko said that Sakura brought her comfort.

Now, her mom said Sakura brought hope.

Was that the red jewel she contained in her chest? Was it hope?

———

The next night, Sakura went to visit her younger brother Takumi in the hospital. She hated how closed in the corridors felt, the too bright lights, the starkness, the chemical smells.

Takumi had been in and out of hospitals for most of his life, though. The doctors would cure whatever was wrong with him, only to have something worse attack.

This might have been the worst scare of all.

However, Takumi had finally stabilized. The doctors

were no longer keeping him in a glass bubble and unconscious. He was in a regular room, now, though he looked as if he'd been attacked by some kind of mechanical spider who had left long wires attached to his arm, his neck, his forehead.

"Hey," Sakura said as she walked into the room. Two other people shared the room. Takumi was in the middle bed, the lucky bed—neither ghosts nor demons could get him there, or so her grandmother had proclaimed earlier when she'd seen him.

Her brother cracked open his eyes. He looked far too pale laying against the white sheets. His black hair was luminous in the dimness.

The patient at the far side of the room was watching a game show at high volume on the TV. The other kid in the bed closest to the door was snoring loudly.

"How can you rest in all this racket?" Sakura teased, taking her brother's hand.

Dark circles lay under his eyes, but Takumi still smiled at her. "You know me. I can sleep anywhere. Even through the zombie apocalypse."

That had been one of their favorite games the past summer—planning out what they'd do in case of a zombie apocalypse. Sakura had not agreed to stashing food around their Tokyo neighborhood as a result, but she still thought about it sometimes.

"Doctors say you're better," Sakura said, squeezing Takumi's hand gently.

He gave a minute shrug. "I guess. It's just…hard, sometimes. Hard to keep going."

"Yeah, well, you can't just die on me," Sakura said firmly. "It would suck if I was the only one left to take care of Mom."

"You're the eldest," Takumi pointed out. "It's always been your responsibility."

"*Shared* responsibility," Sakura said.

It was a frequent argument between them, and one of the things that she always got Takumi to promise, every time he went back into the hospital: that he wouldn't leave her alone to look after Mom.

"Shared," Takumi whispered, nodding. "If I can…"

He gave Sakura a faint smile before he shut his eyes. His hand grew lax in Sakura's.

She knew he still breathed. The machines watched for that sort of thing.

But he was so sick. So ill. He looked so small on the bed. Much worse than usual.

Sakura noticed her hand was turning to glass.

No! No! Not here! Not now! Panicked, Sakura fought back, tried to see her arm as flesh again. She didn't want to give up the feeling of holding her brother's hand in her own.

The transformation paused, then halted.

She felt it grow heavy in her chest.

Maybe she could just change that part of her…

Sakura's hand returned to flesh while her chest blossomed and grew and changed into glass. The red glow seemed deeper, warmer, tonight.

Takumi sighed in his sleep. The lines in his face smoothed out. He looked less tired, suddenly.

Sakura knew she wasn't healing him. That wasn't what the feeling inside her chest told her.

Instead, she was giving him hope that he might survive this latest round.

Sakura sat by Takumi's bedside for a while, before her feet grew restless. She had to go…somewhere else.

As soon as she let go of Takumi's hand, the transformation leapt at her and she changed to glass in an instant.

It was good to know, actually, that she could change that fast. That maybe she had some control over her transformation.

She kissed Takumi's forehead, then tiptoed out of the room though neither of his neighbors had even noted her passing.

Following her feet, Sakura walked up the corridor to the stairs, then up one flight. She didn't know what kind of medicine they practiced here.

But no one questioned her walking the hallway, or peering in patient's rooms. Could they see her? Some people smiled directly at her, but no one shooed her away.

What kind of medicine did they practice here? Hopefully nothing gross or contagious. There seemed to be a mix of both people her age and older adults. Was it a cancer ward? Or just for people who were, like, sick?

Could she catch diseases when she was transformed? That had been a nightmare of hers when she'd been younger, particularly since she'd had to go to the hospital so often because of Takumi.

Normally, Sakura would *die* before walking into some stranger's room. But she couldn't stop herself.

Did she still blush like normal?

An older man lie in the first bed, his black hair tinged with gray along the temples. His bed was sectioned off with curtains from the others. He slept fitfully, like he was having anxious dreams. The monitors beside him silently counted every breath and heartbeat.

Sakura had no idea what was wrong with him.

However, the red jewel in her chest grew brighter in the dim light, coating the curtains in a happy glow.

After a few moments, the man took a deep breath and calmed, the lines in his face smoothing out. He slept better, now. More peaceful.

Had Sakura just restored his hope? She wished she could wake him and ask. But her feet wouldn't let her stay there any longer.

After a while, Sakura got used to walking into stranger's rooms. She never would have believed it. Neither her teachers nor her friends would believe that her, the little mouse, could be so bold.

But she didn't really have a choice. It felt like her feet compelled her, first to an old woman who was so skeletal Sakura was surprised she was still alive, then to a young man weeping beside his father's bed, then to a waiting room where a family held hands and prayed.

She wasn't healing the patients, no, there were too many times when she visited the relatives instead.

She did bring them comfort, however, easing their sleep, their waking, their passing, or their tears.

And maybe, just maybe, she brought them hope.

The next afternoon Sakura lied to Aiko about having to go back to the hospital to visit her brother that night. He was actually doing much better. The plan was for the family to have dinner together, then Sakura could go home or hang out with her friends. Mom knew that Sakura didn't want to spend all her time in the hospital.

However, Sakura found herself reluctant to go be with the girls. What if she turned into glass in front of them?

What if they saw her? What if her feet got restless again? They wouldn't understand. And she wouldn't just be able to leave.

Plus, she'd felt so good going and visiting the sick. She might spend the rest of the night at the hospital again, helping people.

Perhaps this was what she was supposed to do with the red jewel in her chest.

However, Sakura found her feet leading her outside the hospital, then turning left instead of walking straight down the block to the subway station.

Maybe there was another hospital nearby. Other sick people for her to help.

Instead, Sakura found her feet moving swiftly along the sidewalk into Gotanda, one of the worst neighborhoods in Tokyo. The news was always reporting drug busts in the buildings here, or prostitutes being arrested.

She didn't want to go help *those* people. They might hurt her!

The streets were dirty, here. Gross. Garbage piled up in the gutter. Graffiti marred the signposts, the fences, even the sidewalk in places. Sakura jumped every time she heard a loud noise, certain that there would be gunfire soon.

At least people mostly ignored her. Some looked directly at her though, staring rudely. What did they want? What did they *see*? She was too afraid to stop and ask.

Her feet made her turn down a tiny alley. Old scooters littered the edges, more than one in pieces. The door on her left, covered with harsh tags that she suspected were gang markings, looked as though it was locked.

It opened at her touch.

Inside, Sakura wrinkled her nose at the stench of urine and rotten fish. A single bare light bulb lit the dank hallway to her left.

No light shone in the crooked staircase rising in front of her.

But that was where her feet made Sakura go. Up the stairs, quieter than the wind, past the first floor and up to the second.

Most of the walls had been torn out to make one large open space. Bare wood showed where the drywall had rotted off. Hazy smoke from cigarettes gathered near the ceiling and tinted the air blue.

Many people lay on the floor, scattered between the pillars. They huddled under blankets. The one closest to her rocked back and forth muttering.

These people needed hope? Why? How would they use it? Why did she have to do this?

However, Sakura found she couldn't move away, no matter how hard she tried.

Instead, she walked toward the first person. She squirmed with embarrassment when she found herself reaching out and laying her hand on the head of a young man curled up and shivering under a blanket.

His sleep eased. Maybe he could dream sweeter dreams now.

Here, people sometimes burst into tears at Sakura's touch, hope cutting into them deeply. Others she couldn't touch, who glared at her, making her back away. Still others seemed to recognize her in their sleep and reached out to her.

No one tried to hurt her, though. How well could they actually see her? She wasn't sure.

Sakura left after she'd walked through the room twice,

disturbed. This wasn't what she'd imagined spreading hope around would be like. Hope was supposed to be gentle and kind.

But that wasn't what she'd felt at all.

Every night for the next week, Sakura's feet took her to different parts of Tokyo.

Bad parts. Neighborhoods not even tourists would go to.

When Sakura fought her feet, tried not to go, she found herself walking for miles and miles and would still end up in one of those neighborhoods, only she'd be tired and her feet would form blisters that would magically heal by morning.

If she let her feet take her where they wanted to go, she flew through the streets, ending up where she was supposed to be in just a few minutes, her feet surprisingly not tired or sore.

She visited drug dens with junkies sprawled across the floor. Whore houses where the prostitutes were chained to the bed. Girls younger than herself pregnant and homeless.

There were so many, every night. They shared their dreams with her sometimes when she touched them, the bad decisions they'd made.

Sakura tried to give them hope about the future, about the past, about themselves. Enough to help them move on.

One night, after visiting yet another building full of people barely scratching out a living, Sakura heard a child crying.

It was a block away, down a tiny alley, full of litter and graffiti. Her feet didn't make her turn that way, but they didn't turn her away, either.

A young boy sat on the curb about halfway down the alley, bawling his eyes out.

"What's wrong?" Sakura asked. She didn't think the boy needed hope. He needed...something else.

The boy looked up, his eyes still shining with tears. He looked directly at her, which was surprising, since not many did. "Are you the glass lady?" he asked hopefully.

Sakura looked up and down the alley. She didn't see anyone else there. She was still disturbed. "Why do you ask?"

The boy gave a piercing whistle, then hopped up and took off, running into one of the building.

How strange.

When Sakura looked up, now she saw a man at the head of the alley, blocking her exit.

He was tall and skeletal. His bald head glowed in the streetlights. He only had on a cape, he didn't really have huge bat wings, did he?

"Ah, there you are. You know, it's been most amusing trying to keep up with you," the man said.

"Who are you?" Sakura asked, backing up. Was there another way out of the alley? A door that would open to her touch?

But her feet weren't leading her away.

If anything, it seemed as though her feet wanted her to move forward.

"I am Eoki, from the Pandora Society," the man said, bowing his head. "We are here to guide you."

"Pandora...wait," Sakura said. Hadn't she had a test about this recently? "Pandora opened a box so all the evils spilled out into the world, leaving only hope behind."

"Exactly!" Eoki beamed at her, showing all his teeth like a foreigner. "More hope has come into the world, and you bear it, in your *kivotio*."

"My what?" Sakura asked. She was going to have to go look up that word.

"Your glass box, frame, thingy."

If this Eoki was supposed to direct her, or guide her, shouldn't he know more about her? Have a regular name for her glass chest with its ridges? Not just some foreign word?

"So you know about my gift, my abilities," Sakura clarified.

"You woke up one day composed of glass with a red jewel inside," Eoki said with a wave of his hand. "It's now up to us to get that red jewel out so that you can go back to living a normal life again."

That didn't sound right at all. "You can't have it," Sakura said. "I am the bearer of this hope."

"You, my dear, are an overgrown jewelry box who doesn't have a clue of the precious gift you're carrying. How it can be *used*," Eoki said.

"Enlighten me," Sakura said. How *dare* he dismiss her like that? Like all the boys dismissed her? Like her teachers who overlooked her because she was quiet?

"You see, spread just a little bit of that hope around our advertisements, and we make billions of Yen selling supplements and unnecessary medical goods!" Eoki said cheerfully. "Or better yet, mail it off to a bunch of investors. Let them speculate like mad in the market. There are so many uses for this hope of yours."

"That's not true hope," Sakura said. "That's...twisting people's hope. Their dreams."

Eoki sighed. "I told the society that we needed to scoop you up sooner, like the other Hopes. It would give you too many ideas, I told them. But no. They wanted you to develop more, for your hope to grow stronger, so it would last longer after we extract it from you."

Sakura shivered. She knew that she wouldn't survive this "extraction."

"So come along now," Eoki said.

"No," Sakura said.

"'No'?" Eoki asked, smirking. "You sound like a three year old. Stomping your foot when you've been told its time to go to bed. Your hope may be stronger than the others, but it's still weak. Frail. You can't escape."

Sakura looked at her arms with their sharp ridges. It was true, she was made of glass. She would break someday, and all the hope she carried would dribble out over the sidewalk, into the gutter as she passed away.

"Hope isn't timid," Sakura told Eoki. "It visits the worst of the slums."

Sakura took a step forward, her voice gaining strength. "Hope isn't shy. It touches strangers and friends alike."

She raised one of her arms up in front of her, across her chest. "And hope can cut like a knife when it's unexpected."

Sakura *rushed* at Eoki, moving with all the speed her feet would give her. Then she slashed out with her arm, bashing him across the face.

Eoki stumbled back, his cheek bleeding, his face in complete shock.

"You pervert hope," Sakura said, stalking forward. "And you are poorer for it."

Eoki shook his head one more time before his stood up straighter. "I *told* them it was a bad idea to leave you alone for so long. But don't worry. I'll be back. With reinforcements."

With that, Eoki swirled away on a great black cloud, smelling of burnt dreams.

Sakura stood alone at the head of the alley. He'd be back? And he'd bring more people to attack her? She was all alone. Most people couldn't even *see* her when she'd transformed into glass.

The jewel in Sakura's chest pulsed once, turning the whole street a happy, cheery red.

Eoki would come back, and keep coming back, until finally he defeated Sakura.

But that wouldn't happen for a long, long while.

Because while Sakura might be alone, she had hope.

AUTHOR'S NOTES

I wrote this story for a workshop. While the original editor didn't take the story, a second one liked it enough to buy it, so it came out in an "Editor's Choice" collection that year, the so-called left over stories from the workshop that didn't sell to their intended markets.

One of the reasons I included this story is because of a review that it received. *Tangent Online* called it "surprisingly deep urban fantasy." (It was also listed as one of their top twenty-five stories for that year.)

I have always liked that phrase—surprisingly deep urban fantasy. I think I write a lot of that. While a story might superficially be just entertaining, at least in my stories, there's a lot more going on.

THE THIRD RAVEN

Pedrek pulled his long raven cloak tighter across his shoulders. The wind blew more coarsely here, high on the cliffs overlooking the town of Sulwyn. Pedrek wondered if it was an omen, the cold wind foretelling a chilly reception in the town below.

They wouldn't deny him entrance, of course. The wood and earthworks surrounding the town couldn't stop him, and though they didn't get many of his kind up here, they might even make him welcome, at least at the start. The novelty of a visiting raven warrior had gotten him two or three nights' stay for free in other small villages. Maybe there was work here as well—bandits, unscrupulous tax collectors, or even a rotten Lowen or spell-worker—that the town would pay for Pedrek to clean up.

The steep roofs below told Pedrek the snow likely to come in the winter. He'd be long gone before it came, going south if he could, to islands where ice never clipped his wings. It would be a long, cold winter without Ebril, his mate. He sighed and looked out again.

A river coursed through the far edge of the town, next to the hills, large enough for merchants and their ships. From Pedrek's high perch, the town looked peaceful and prosperous, just the kind of place he needed, at least for a while.

Harsh winds pushed at Pedrek, whipping the edges of his cloak. He should just leave now; give into the change and fly true. He stubbornly kept off his wings and instead returned to the trail, stomping the dirt with his very human feet, reminding his feathered soul that his human half had needs as well: companionship, cooked meat, warm fires, and four walls of safety at night. And maybe a few more coins to line his purse: Ebril had been sick a long time, but none of the expensive spells or potions had worked.

As Pedrek drew closer to the town he realized the earthworks hadn't been maintained: They crumbled on the sides and the main gateway sagged. No one challenged him as he walked up the road. Likely there would be no work here for him, either. He'd just stay the night then, and continue his travels in the morning. He only needed a few more shiny coins before heading south.

Pedrek was used to the stares he received in small villages like this. He kept his back straight as he marched toward the piers, figuring any inns would be near there.

What Pedrek hadn't expected was how startled the people seemed, pointing and whispering as he passed. He wondered what a previous member of the raven clan had done to garnish so much attention.

Before Pedrek got to the river, an old grandmother put herself directly in his path. "Have you come for Corin?" she demanded. Though she only came up to Pedrek's chest, her fierceness matched that of the great mountain cat he'd seen defending her young. "Finally going to take care of your own?"

"For who?" Pedrek asked.

"Figured. Mighty raven warriors," she said disdainfully. "This way," she added, walking the direction Pedrek had been going, toward the water.

"What do you mean?" Pedrek asked. Raven warriors were usually treated with fear or drudging respect. Not dismissed by grandmothers with curls arranged by the wind and faces covered in wrinkles.

"This way," was the only response he received.

Not two blocks away, on the boardwalk of inns and shops that faced the water, the old woman stopped and merely pointed. "There," she said, spitting once before stomping away.

Mystified, Pedrek walked toward the shop she'd indicated, not seeing the boy until he was much closer.

Most of the raven clans manifested their human side with shock white or silver hair, nearly colorless eyes, and tanned skin. This boy had raven dark hair and eyes. He stood in the shadows, the sun casting wan light on his pale face. He wore the brightest white shirt Pedrek had ever seen.

It wasn't until the boy moved—Corin, Pedrek assumed—that Pedrek saw what else the shadows had hidden.

Instead of two arms, the boy only had one.

The other was a raven's wing, black as a nightmare.

Pedrek shivered, but bit his tongue, refusing to name his fear: half-breed.

———

"What happened?" Pedrek finally asked after the pair of them had stared at each other for long moments. Maybe people passed them on the boardwalk, but Pedrek didn't pay attention to them, keeping all his focus on the boy.

Corin looked like he was about to take flight, but he stayed. "Cursed," he said. He jerked his chin at the cloak Pedrek wore. "Is that what they're supposed to do? Turn into a cloak you can carry around?"

"No," Pedrek admitted. It was a popular myth, one that the raven clan didn't discourage too much, giving the warriors more mystique. "It's primarily just a cloak."

The boy seemed disappointed. "So it can't help me change all the way back?"

Pedrek shook his head. "But maybe I can help."

Corin scoffed. "Told you I was cursed. I need some kind of magic. Not mere words about listening to my feathered soul."

"Do you talk with your feathered soul?" Pedrek asked.

"No such thing," Corin declared, staring at him.

Pedrek blinked, surprised. Corin was old enough—at least seven, he guessed—that the boy should have had contact from his feathered half. "Who cursed you?"

"Old Lowen up in the hills," the boy said, looking at the ground.

Pedrek was certain the boy lied, but he wasn't sure about what. "Who taught you about the raven clan?"

"Ma did. She'd known about them."

"She's dead?" Pedrek asked, wanting to be clear.

"Yes." Corin looked up and glared. "Might not have been the same old Lowen, but it had to be something like that. She just—wasted away. As if something ate her from the inside out."

That time Pedrek knew the boy spoke the truth. "Did she ever make plans for you? Arrangements to go into the guard?"

"No, why would she?"

"It's tradition," Pedrek replied. "And you need it—you need the teachings of Raven's Hall for your raven soul."

"But I'd have to leave here!" Corin exclaimed.

"Don't you want to?" Pedrek asked, looking around. The river offered some open air, but there were still too many buildings, too many people. He was already longing for clear skies.

The boy shook his head, puzzled.

Pedrek suddenly was struck by how the boy may have been cursed: The Lowen witch hadn't stolen his arm, or left him halfway between states. It wasn't anything as obvious as that.

No, she'd stolen the boy's raven soul, and left merely a wing in its place.

———

Pedrek had been born in a town far to the south and west. His father had been a well-known warrior, lost in a battle just after Pedrek had been born. Mama sold the lamps she and her sisters made out of pottery. Pedrek helped dab designs into the soft clay, his tiny fingers making patterns around the pouring hole. He loved making his own shapes, and if he hadn't been born so blond and tan, maybe he would have become a potter, too.

On one particular day, when Pedrek was maybe four or five, he'd been playing in the back of the market stall all morning. He was too little to help Mama, but too big to be strapped to her back all day. He'd found a line of ants to play with. He used a stick to divert the line, making them march around the obstacle. Then he got two sticks and tried to make them march down between them, but they kept crawling over the sticks, keeping to their line.

When one crawled over Pedrek's fingers, he brought it closer so he could see it better. Its antenna waved a lot and it marched across his hand, looking for something to eat, Pedrek assumed.

Pedrek was suddenly hungry as well. He looked at Mama, busy with a temple buyer, haggling over a sack of lamps. Then he looked at the ant.

Something Pedrek had never felt before pushed at him. *Do it,* it whispered.

Peter flicked out his tongue and easily picked up the ant, swallowing it whole.

More, said that quiet voice.

By the time Mama looked over, Pedrek had eaten a dozen ants or more.

"What are you doing?" Mama squawked, grabbing Pedrek by the arm, lifting him off the ground and shaking him. "You're not supposed to eat ants!"

Pedrek, ashamed, looked down at his chubby fingers, at the ant bodies crushed between them, a few ants still blazing trails across his palms. He suddenly felt sick to his stomach.

"Ma'am." A stranger called to them from the stall counter. He was a blond as Pedrek. "Is he raven-get?"

"Oh, lord, yes," Mama said, brushing the remaining ants from Pedrek's hands with an edge of her skirt.

"He's ready for the training," the man continued.

"He's—he's young," Mama said, kneeling and looking Pedrek in the eye. She pushed the hair off his forehead, then cupped his cheek. Pedrek leaned into the contact, comforted that while Mama was still mad, she didn't seem to be that angry.

Pedrek wanted Mama to keep looking at him, like he was all she saw, because when she turned away she looked both frightened and sad.

"No younger than I was," the stranger said. "You must send him to the guard. Before he hurts himself."

Mama nodded then crushed Pedrek to her, holding him tight. She didn't let go all the rest of the day, holding his hand or cradling him close. That night, though he had his own pile of blankets, Mama let him crawl up into her big bed.

The next morning, the guard came, and it was a year before Pedrek saw Mama again.

"Can you help me?" Corin demanded.

Pedrek slowly nodded. "Yes. But we'll have to go see the old Lowen."

"Why?" Corin looked wary.

"I think she stole something from you," Pedrek admitted. "We need to get it back." He didn't want to admit exactly what just yet.

"Really?" Corin asked, suspicious and skeptical. "Why would she listen to you when she wouldn't even talk with anyone else?"

"Did any of them accuse her of stealing something specific of yours?" Pedrek countered.

Corin shook his head. His human hand reached across his chest and he slowly stroked the feathers of his raven arm, thinking.

"Then we will go see her in the morning," Pedrek announced. "Now—you need to help me. Which inn should I stay at tonight?"

Corin led Pedrek a few blocks off the piers, walking along the high boardwalks to avoid the mud and muck of the street. The buildings were all wood, no brick or stone. The town was prosperous; Pedrek could tell by the number of specialty stores, not just a general mercantile but cloth, leather, and lamp vendors. The buildings were all wood, no brick or stone, with high, steep roofs and murals of folktales painted on the walls.

Pedrek booked a bed for two nights. Brae the

innkeeper only charged him for one. "You do well for our Corin there and maybe I'll drop a few more coins off."

"Thank you," Pedrek said, surprised. The room was a dorm with six cots. The wooden floors were clear of mud and the mattress smelled clean. It wasn't as clean as any room in Raven's Hall, but Pedrek was used to that now. He dropped his pack and spread the raven cloak over it. Most wouldn't dare touch his belongings, afraid of spells that didn't exist. All Pedrek did was smooth his palm over the feathers, leaving some of his raven's awareness behind. If anyone did bother his things, he'd at least have a clear impression of him, her, or it.

Satisfied, Pedrek went back to the common room. A fireplace dominated the shorter wall, with a working hearth. A pole ran from the floor to the roof of the firebox, arranged with several iron arms that could swing over the fire for cooking, then back into the room for serving. Long tables with benches filled the floor. When he'd been younger, he'd often just slept in the common room of whatever inn he stayed at. Now his older bones appreciated a mattress. A tall bar stood in the other corner, next to the door. Pedrek put in his order for dinner as well as a pint of a local beer before sitting down at the main table.

Pedrek didn't have to wait long until other patrons started to file in. Loud conversation filled the room and the scents of a spicy fish stew wafted from the hearth. Pedrek primarily listened to his companions, trying to spot ones who would talk with him.

After he'd eaten, he went up to the bar, ordered three pints, then sat down next to the two best candidates. They both thanked him with a grunt, a silent toast, and a long drink.

"Here for Corin?" asked the older man with silver hair. He had a rough, scrubbed face, as if the wind had scoured it and left it ruddy and pale.

"Yes," Pedrek said. "Was looking to hear any tales of his da." He knew Corin's mother had been a local, and knew better than to ask about her, especially since she was dead.

"Not much to tell," said the other. He was darker, with dirty blond hair and hazel eyes. "He wasn't here long, two or three weeks maybe."

"Really?" Pedrek asked, surprised. Most members of the raven clan mated once, and for life. "What happened?"

The men shifted and the quiet grew between them, until the first man spoke again. "Some say Morna's father ran him off. Others claim it was the old Lowen, the same as cursed the boy."

"He wasn't driven off," Pedrek said with certainty. None of the raven clan would have left his mate behind, no matter how hastily the match had been made. He wondered if it had just been a boy passing through, practicing his mating techniques and not expecting to be answered so quickly.

Pedrek took a deep draught when he had another thought: Had the Lowen stolen that young man's soul as well? "What can you tell me of the Lowen?"

"She lives up Red Peak, near the pass. Some of the women in town use her as a healer." Both men took large drinks, as if washing the taste from their mouths.

"Could she have had an earlier incident with Morna?" Pedrek asked finally, hoping the men wouldn't take it wrong.

"She swore she only went up the once, to confront the Lowen after what happened to Corin. Came back more pale than a three-day frost. Wouldn't hear of anyone else going back up," the first man confided, nodding seriously.

The darker man scoffed. "Of course that didn't stop some fools. Marched up the hill and got lost for days before they made their way back. Men *born* here," he emphasized. "Lowen can't be found if she doesn't want to be."

"Think she'll see me?"

The two men considered the question so long Pedrek feared they wouldn't actually form an answer. Finally, as one, both men drained their pints and stood.

"Aye. She'll be curious enough to see you," said the first.

"Just make sure you see her, too," said the other. Then the pair of them turned and walked out the inn, leaving Pedrek to ponder their words alone for the rest of the night.

The first prevailing fact young Pedrek noticed when he came to Raven Hall was the warmth: Each walkway and room had either a fireplace or a stove. Window wells and walls wore blankets so drafts couldn't get in. Candle stands stood beside each desk in the classroom so no one took a chill.

Pedrek's raven soul basked in the tropical, sheltering heat. Though the youngest students were frequently seated farthest from the flames, Pedrek never really felt cold.

The next omnipresent fact about the hall was the writing. Every student, no matter what age they entered, learned their letters. Not just to read, but to write as well, diligently marking up clay tablets or using chalk on freshly cleaned slates. Day after day they learned until all in Pedrek's class could be called literate.

The third fact, which Pedrek never mentioned to another soul even decades after he'd left the hall, were the recitations. They'd started simply enough: Every student had to write down the verse their tutor said, quickly and correctly. When they'd reached a certain accuracy their tutor announced a guest visitor.

Old prefect Aderyn stomped her way to the head of the classroom, leaning heavily on a cane. One eye stared at them, clear as morning skies. The other was merely a hole, empty and scarred with black skin and red veins. She wore a misshapen gown, and it was whispered it hid other deformities.

Aderyn thumped her cane to make sure everyone in the class was paying attention. She announced the recitation and waited a moment while students got ready.

Into the poised still air, Aderyn began a different recitation, one the children had never heard before but would hear many times afterward.

"I will not eat bugs or insects."

A couple of boys sniggered. Aderyn silenced them with a thump of her cane. "I will not eat bugs or insects," she repeated.

Pedrek felt nauseous suddenly, but he wrote out all the words.

"I will not eat the dead mice in the yard," Aderyn recited next.

The older student at the end of the bench shifted nervously in his seat. Pedrek exchanged glances with his friend beside him. They'd both heard the rumor, of course, but none of the younger ones had dared asked what had actually happened.

"I will not eat animals rotting in fields or forests," Aderyn instructed.

Pedrek wrinkled his nose. He found this one easier than the first two. He'd never do such a thing, he was certain.

"I will not eat the dead."

The words rang ominously through the hall.

"I will not haunt the battlefield or feast on human flesh."

Pedrek shivered and tried to write the words down, though his raven soul stirred now, needling him for attention.

"I will not pluck out a corpse's eyes," Aderyn announced to the now silent classroom. She stared at them, her one remaining eye unblinking. "Because that corpse might rise up to slaughter me like the half-breed I am." No one even pretended to keep writing, the words ringing terrible and true.

Half-breed was the worst insult the children could fling at one another. It meant someone who wasn't fully human or raven and who had their human and raven souls misaligned; half here, half there, and never truly whole.

"I will not suffer the half-breed."

The morning brought winds that promised snow before night. The cold made Pedrek draw his cloak tighter across his shoulders as they started up Red Peak. Corin didn't seem to notice the bite in the air: either he was too used to the cold or too excited. Possibly both.

They followed rutted dirt roads out of town, passing from the boardwalks to the ground, detouring around wide frozen puddles. The lands stayed pretty even as they passed the fall fields, barren but fringed with trees still holding their colors.

Pedrek tried to talk with Corin, but the boy had lost much of his brashness from the day before. As they took their first break from walking steadily up the hill, Pedrek asked, "So what really happened with the Lowen?"

Corin's scowl returned. "She cursed me. What else do you need to know?"

Pedrek shook his head. "She stole something. And I still don't know why. Or why your mother didn't fight harder to get it back."

"What do you mean?" Corin asked, worried. "She fought. She fought really hard."

The uncertainty of Corin's claims echoed around them. "No, she didn't, and you know why," Pedrek accused the boy.

Corin pressed his lips together and mulishly raised his chin. After treating Pedrek to a few moments of silent glaring, Corin finally muttered, "Doesn't matter. You'll likely find out soon enough." He refused to say anything more, but marched away, back up the hill.

As they walked further away from the trees crowding the road and back into true hills with craggy rocks, Pedrek longed to take wing. He wanted to float up and see the cliffs from afar. His legs ached from constantly climbing and the silence of the boy chafed him. However, he dared not leave Corin, and he wasn't sure how the old Lowen would react to his raven form.

Just before midday, the road veered to the right. Corin picked the trail to the left, across the face of the peak. It was clear and flat, a welcome change to the winding road they'd been following.

The trail suddenly ran into a large grove of trees. Pedrek saw a glimmer and stopped Corin with a hand on his arm. "I should go first now," Pedrek said, drawing Corin behind him. He took a few steps, then realized the boy had stopped. He turned to look.

Corin stood in the center of the trail with his human arm akimbo and his head tilted to the side.

Pedrek's soul lifted. It was the first birdlike gesture Corin had made.

"Why are you all fluffed up like that?" Corin finally asked, his human hand gesturing toward Pedrek's cloak.

"There's some sort of magic there," Pedrek said, indicating the trees.

"Where?" Corin said, staying where he was but staring hard at the trees.

"You're young yet," Pedrek lied. "Too young to see." Corin's raven soul should have detected the charm in the trees, though it wouldn't have been trained to identify it: a simple spell to make the location seem darker and more ominous.

Corin looked a bit more, then shook his head, crestfallen. "Her place is just through there," he said, indicating the trees.

"Are you frightened of the woods?" Pedrek asked.

"Of course not," Corin claimed boldly.

"If you think they're dark while we're walking through them, you should touch my cloak," Pedrek told him. It didn't have a lot of magic, but just enough that might clear the boy's vision.

Midway through the trees, Pedrek felt cautious fingers along his back.

"This is better," Corin admitted softly after a few more steps.

Pedrek merely nodded and kept walking.

The trail opened up into a fair meadow. The grass shone summer green, the winter-weighted wind calmed, and the sun shone clear and blue. Conifers circled the meadow, dark prickly guardians. A tiny creek burbled across the center, and on the far side stood a picturesque white cottage.

Charms twinkled here, too. Pedrek recognized the ones to increase the beauty and bring calm, but the others were too advanced for him. He would have little recourse if it came to a battle of magic.

As they walked across a figure exited the cottage and began toward them. Pedrek knew it had to be the Lowen, but she appeared to be a young girl. Given the warnings from the night before, Pedrek stopped and asked his raven soul to help. The squawked reply came so quickly and so loudly it startled him, causing him to shake once from head to toe.

When Pedrek's vision had cleared, he looked around again. Most of the color had bled out of the day. The charms lost their sparkle, and instead, seemed like dull dolls made out of hair, yarn, and twigs. The woman approaching them now looked stooped and ancient. Pedrek stared at her. She met his gaze from across the meadow and gave him a death's-head grin.

A tug on his cloak made Pedrek swing around. It was merely Corin though. "Your eyes are black," Corin exclaimed.

"Yes," Pedrek replied, the word coming out in a birdlike croak. He cleared his throat and pushed back. He needed his human voice. "Yes," he said again, stronger this time. "Let's go meet the Lowen and find out where's she's hidden your raven soul."

The boy looked startled by Pedrek's declaration, then threw his shoulders back, determined, marching across the field, raising first a human arm, then a raven's wing, in time with his feet.

Pedrek threw a quick prayer to both Wynne, goddess of the ravens, as well as Tamsin, god of lost causes.

"I know why you've come," the old Lowen cackled from her side of the creek. "And I'm not changing him back." She wore a patchwork quilt as a cloak, spells woven into each section. A bright blue wimple captured most of her iron gray hair, but long wisps still hung down beside her face. Her eyes matched the blue of the wimple, as piercing as a summer sky. She leaned heavily on a stout cane, the head gnarled and rubbed smooth with age.

"Why did you take his raven soul?" Pedrek asked, determined to be as polite as he could be. He knew he could still escape if it grew nasty, but he'd never get the boy away unharmed.

"So those eyes see more than just worms," the old woman muttered. "He didn't know how to control it," she accused, indicating Corin with her chin. "Came up here and caused mischief most every day. Wouldn't stay away."

"He was just a boy, not even a teen," Pedrek pointed out reasonably. "No one had trained him yet."

"Because you always care for your own, right?" the Lowen said, pointing her cane at Pedrek. "None of you even knew he was here."

"If his father had lived until he'd been born, we would have known. And someone would have come," Pedrek insisted.

"'Twasn't me who shot the fool," the Lowen growled. "Idiot hunters from the other side of the pass had done it for sport, then come running to me when the bird turned into a man on the ground."

"Why didn't you say anything to his wife?" Pedrek demanded.

"Weren't married now, were they?" the woman asked slyly. "They'd just been playing house. Didn't know about it for years, until his young'un come to pester me."

"He needs to be whole," Pedrek insisted.

"Not gonna give it back," the Lowen said, crossing her arms across her chest and staring hard at him.

"Why not?" Pedrek asked into the growing stillness on the hill. Even the bird song from the nearby trees had died. "What happened? What did he do?"

"He won't tell you?" the Lowen asked.

Pedrek shook his head.

Corin turned his back on both of them.

"Got hungry while him and his friends were playing, didn't he? Had a knight here, proper warrior of the king. Had done what I could to save him, but he'd been brought to me too late."

Pedrek had to swallow hard against the sudden dryness in his throat. "Go on," he directed her, though he didn't want to hear the rest.

"This one and his two friends decided to snack on the body. By the time I came back the other two had snagged his eyeballs, and this one, his tongue."

Pedrek held himself very still, reminding himself that Corin hadn't been taught his letters or his recitations, hadn't been schooled about his raven soul, didn't know how to placate it.

Corin wasn't a half-breed.

"Now, I don't blame critters for doing what they're born to do, but he knew better," the Lowen finished, pointing at Corin.

"I did not!" Corin said hotly, turning around. "I thought it was fine when I was a raven!"

"He was never trained," Pedrek said. "His human soul knew better, but couldn't share that."

The old Lowen shook her head. "He knew. He sat and laughed at me, daring me to do something after I chased his friends away."

"He didn't know," Pedrek maintained, unsure if he spoke the truth. It was possibly Corin's raven soul had known, but just not cared.

The first time Pedrek saw battle, neither his human or raven soul rejoiced. There was too much fear, too much nervous exhilaration, too much boredom, and then, finally, too much dirt and blood. It was impossible to know who'd won the first skirmish. After the violent clash both sides were allowed to treat their wounded and carry away their dead.

Everyone had looked strangely at Pedrek when he'd volunteered to help clear the field. He'd been paired with an older man named Reece, who had bright cooper curls and white skin covered in freckles. They carried corpses between them on a stretcher, stacked two and three high.

"He working all right?" people asked every time they came back with a full load. To which Reece always cheerfully replied that he'd only thrown up once, which was kind, because Pedrek had had to stop more than once to settle his stomach.

"Why do they keep asking that?" Pedrek said after the third time.

"Your kind tend to stay away after the fighting," Reece told him with a grin. "Seeing the state of your stomach, I can see why."

Pedrek nodded, not bothering to tell Reece the truth. The recitations had been drilled into him, into every person in the raven clan. He didn't fear breaking those laws: his human and raven selves were better aligned than that. The reason he'd volunteered was because he'd still had to *know* what it felt like to be so close to the newly dead. His raven soul had awakened hungry, but Pedrek had soothed it with visions of clear skies, promising a good long flight the next day, as well as digging out the shiny glass beads hidden at the bottom of his pack and keeping those under his pillow that night.

As the night grew longer and fewer men moved about the field, scavengers came. Reece and Pedrek worked as quickly as they could, but they were always shooing them away.

More than once Pedrek recognized the birds.

The next day Pedrek went to the chief of his line. "I volunteered last night to help clear the dead."

"I heard. Good man," the chief exclaimed. Then he paused. "Ah. You're curious about the ones who visited the dead not in human form."

Pedrek nodded, angry and afraid.

"You'll see. We always take care of our own, son."

Before the last battle, Pedrek noticed that only one of those who'd eaten the dead were still alive. He didn't know if it was fate or the chief's hand directing the others into the heat of battle. Pedrek searched out the one who remained, finding him looking out over the field as if he were already dead. "Why did you do it? Break the recitation?" Pedrek hissed at him quietly.

The man shrugged and looked at him with all black eyes. "Don't care," he squawked.

A welcoming nod came from Pedrek's own raven's soul. It didn't care, either. However, it let itself be consoled with smaller things because it did care for Pedrek in its own, small way.

"The boy is my responsibility now," Pedrek told the Lowen. The beautiful summer day had grown cold and clouds now covered the once-clear sky. Wind coursed through the trees surrounding them, tossing the heads of the pines.

The old Lowen's eyes grew crafty. "You'll take him with you?"

"I will," Pedrek vowed. "I swear by my raven's soul."

"So you do take care of your own."

"You'd take me with you?" Corin asked.

"To Raven's Hall. You must be trained," Pedrek said, intending to get the boy the help he needed. Belatedly, he remembered Corin only had a single soul. "You might be able to come back later."

"I don't want to leave," Corin said. "But if she gives me my raven's soul again, I can learn to be a warrior like you?"

The Lowen snorted, but Pedrek nodded solemnly. "Yes, most of the raven clan earn their keep, hiring out as warriors for a while."

"Then yes, I'll go with you," Corin said. He finally turned and addressed the old Lowen. "Please."

"Ah, didn't think you knew that word," she said. She lifted one side of her quilt, reached into a deep pocket and pulled out a raven-black egg. A golden web of strings bound it tightly. "Here," she said, tossing it to the boy. "Swallow it."

Corin glanced wide-eyed at Pedrek, who nodded. He suspected the Lowen wouldn't hurt the boy now that Pedrek had promised to take him away. The boy was now his responsibility, and the raven clan did take care of their own.

"Do as she says," Pedrek told Corin as he continued to hesitate.

With one last shudder, Corin closed his eyes, opened his mouth, and shoved the egg inside.

The egg collapsed as soon as it touched his tongue, flowing dark and pure out of the eggshell, down Corin's throat as well as out of his mouth. It dribbled down his chin and across his shoulder to the one raven's wing. The droplets sucked the darkness into themselves as they rolled down, leaving a pale boy's arm behind.

Corin's hair also grew pale, and when he opened his eyes, they'd changed to the color of morning mist. After his raven's soul had settled, only a shock of black hair remained, dripping over Corin's eyes.

"Thank you," Pedrek told the old Lowen, heartfelt and warm. It was good to see the boy whole.

Corin lifted first one arm then the other, staring at all ten fingers.

"Don't be thanking me yet," the Lowen cackled. A cloud quickly gathered around her. The next moment, she was gone.

"Where did she go?" Corin asked, looking around, seeming frightened.

"Away," Pedrek assured him.

"I'm glad you chased her away," the boy told him before taking a running leap into the air and changing into his raven form, leaving his clothes behind.

"I didn't chase her anywhere," Pedrek muttered. "And I'm not chasing you, either," he added after he picked up the clothes and began walking back to the trees.

By the time Pedrek had reached the road, Corin had joined him in human form. The natural grace of the raven clan had returned and Corin walked light on his feet. After he dressed, he still shivered. Pedrek had him walk beside him so they could share the warmth of his cloak.

Before they reached the town, Corin had started listing every sight in the kingdom that he just had to see.

"Won't you miss here?" Pedrek asked softly.

Corin looked up toward the darkening sky. "I—we—don't belong here."

"Then let's go tomorrow," Pedrek replied, getting a bright smile in return.

That night, under not just piles of blankets but his cloak as well, Pedrek slept deeply, dreaming of open blue skies and easy meat.

They left town quickly, both of them anxious to get on the road. More than one of the locals shook Pedrek's hand as a thank-you for taking care of their Corin.

Corin promised to visit when he could, though Pedrek made certain that he made no such vows. He knew Corin meant well, and maybe he'd fulfill them.

Pedrek remembered how awkward it was every time he'd visited Mama after he'd gone into the guard. How little she knew of the world while the ravens shared news from all the different kingdoms, even those across the sea. Their old house was so cold compared to Raven's Hall, and dirty as well. Growing up he'd never been aware of how many bugs shared their quarters; after the recitations, he couldn't think of anything else.

Their packs were fully loaded with dried meat, bread, and cheese, their flasks were full when they started their journey. As they walked, Pedrek encouraged Corin to regain his raven form, fly, and save his feet. Pedrek even carried Corin sometimes, a squawking bird on his shoulder or nestled under his cloak.

Every night, by the light of the fire, Pedrek made Corin draw letters in the soft dirt. He knew he had to rush things for Corin, so he also started with the simplest of the recitations as well. He could never be as impressive as Aderyn, but he did his best to impress Corin how important it was to not eat human flesh. He made the boy repeat the lessons until he'd memorized every line. As a reward, he answered Corin's questions about being a warrior, cleaning up some of his battle stories. There were a few that had been more exciting than terrifying.

As they reached the rolling hills that spread out into the flatlands, the wind carried the scent of lime, decay, and dark spells.

When Corin asked about it, Pedrek didn't think to lie. "It's the smell of battle. At least a few days old."

"Can we go? Can we see? I've never seen a battle before."

"All right," Pedrek said, pushing down on his anxiety, telling himself that it was merely the thrill of the battle, not the lure of the corpses that was drawing Corin.

On the far side of a scorched field, workers still buried

the dead in a long trench. Healing tents sat not too far off, with only a few soldiers remaining behind. Pedrek hadn't been asking the local birds for the news; he vowed to do so in the morning, see if there were roads or lands ahead that weren't safe for him and a boy.

That night, the sound of wings woke Pedrek. Corin had changed form and gone.

It was easy enough for Pedrek to get to the battlefield quicker than Corin, a touch of magic aiding his flight. He waited in human form for Corin to arrive, hoping he'd been wrong. He had to breathe out harshly as the raven delightedly tore into the waiting flesh, playing with entrails and flapping skin.

When Pedrek could finally control himself, after he'd quieted his raven's soul enough, he stepped into the opening. "Come here, Corin," he called softly.

The boy was still young. He didn't recognize the glimmer in Pedrek's hand as the enticing magic it was. He hopped his way over to Pedrek, then looked at him, tilting his head one way, then the other.

Pedrek kept his movements steady and gentle, bending down to give the bird a lift up, stroking its body tenderly, whispering to it, "It's all right. It's all right."

Before he suddenly snapped the raven's neck.

The next morning another grave had joined the others on the battlefield, and Pedrek continued his journey by himself.

The raven clan always took care of their own.

AUTHOR'S NOTES

This was another story that I wrote as part of the *Baker's Dozen* challenge. In the original author's notes for this story, I wrote about how I could easily set a novel in this world. Not that I necessarily would have, but the world was so developed in my head that I could have.

As it was the next to last story that I wrote for the challenge, I never went back and wrote more stories about these particular characters.

However, as part of a writing exercise for a workshop, I decided to take these characters and bring them forward, into the modern era.

That became the first chapter for *The Raven and the Dancing Tiger*, the first of the Shadow Wars trilogy. And that is partially why I'm including this story, as it shows how I took a basic idea and twisted it into something different.

GRACIE'S FIRE

Mother-of-a-whore my boots hurt. They pinched my toes, chafed my ankles, and the damn heels made my back and calves ache. The best part of every night was finally getting home to the garret above the feed shop and taking 'em off. Even if they was a present from my long-lost husband, god bless his soul, made outta solid black leather with brass hooks and laces, they felt like they was taking orders from the devil himself.

I still wore 'em with a smile. I even practiced walking as gracefully as I could, from one end of The Gold Mine Saloon to the other, across the sawdust and straw-strewn floor, balancing my tray with one hand, like they did at the Barstow Hotel, in the fancy part of town. They did make my hips sway, which garnered attention and more tips. Tips that I saved, tips that were gonna get me out of that garret and maybe buy me my own piece of land someday.

Not that I was likely to get any tips tonight. The saloon was deader than a priest's cell on a Saturday night. The seven-twenty train from Sacramento wasn't coming in: bridge had flooded out (again). As we was directly across the muddy street from the train station, it brought us most of our trade.

As for folks from here in Stockton, well, Lucky Lucy's had just opened down the street—and they had dancing girls.

Mister Thomas didn't much approve of them. He didn't make us strip down to nothing either. I couldn't have worn my dress to church, but it only bared my shoulders, ankles, and arms. I kinda liked the color too, a rich gold across my chest that didn't show the dirt too much, over a black short-sleeved blouse and a hitched up skirt. It showed off that pale Irish skin of mine, and Mister

Thomas said the gold matched my green eyes. Nothing worked with my hair of course—I wore it shamefully short, and it was too thick and black to be much use.

The only "special" that The Gold Mine Saloon had to offer was that hulking steam-powered contraption that took up half the bar, another one of Mister Thomas' inventions. Me and the girls done made him get rid of most of thems: the weird, flickering, automatic lights (we all preferred gaslight); the odd moving belt for taking the dishes back to the kitchen (it was nice of him to try and save us some steps, but the pile ups and broken glassware made all our lives hell); and the clockwork automaton that used to run the drink machine (Mister Thomas said it wasn't alive, and its eyes was just glass, but it'd still watch all the girls walk around the saloon, giving us chills).

We had traditional kegs of beer, bottles of cheap whisky, and cheap moonshine—cloudy liquid in big bottles that'd eat anything, even brass, if we tried cleaning with it. I coulda made better, but Mister Tomas didn't want to get into the distilling business, not like that.

However, the machine, well, it could make pretty much any drink. Large glass jars of colored liquid—pink, brown, green, blue, and yellow—stuck out of one end of the sleek brass, like a peacock's tail. At least a dozen knobs, wheels, and gears regulated the flow and temperature of the liquid as it churned through the machine. The twisting spigot on the other end looked like glass, but it was hard as diamond.

That contraption could make damn near anything. Fizzy, sparkling lemonade that tasted like the perfect summer day. Dark, rich wine that reminded you of Mama's stews in deep winter. That odd, blue drink that left smoke on your tongue and tears in your eyes.

A lot of the locals didn't care much for the machine, never buying drinks from it. But sometimes a riverboat hand or a farmer'd get drunk, tell me to make 'em whatever I felt like.

I always got a good tip from that.

Sometimes stupid cowpokes would come in, drunk already, then dare each other to come up with wilder concoctions, and force 'em down.

Then I'd have to shove 'em out the door before they started puking.

Tonight, though, no one was ordering nothing. Mister Thomas was at his regular weekly poker game—the one I'd rescued him from at least twice over the years—and had left me in charge for the night, as usual. Old Dusky sat at the bar, nursing his customary one whisky. He were a regular, but rarely talked. Just sat, had his one drink, drawing patterns on the bar with his finger. Two businessmen sat in one corner, talking about some land deal they was putting together.

And that was it.

I'd already sent all the other girls home, so it was just me behind the long bar. Me in those damn boots that I daydreamed about burning in the grate at the far end of the saloon. I'd set my mind to close the bar early—kick Dusky out and start moving the businessmen along—when the doors swung open and in came this group of four men.

Well, at first I thought they was men. They was in these big black cloaks with the hoods up, shapeless and hiding their faces. But they were regular height, and didn't look too wide, either.

"Gentlemen," I called out. "We're clos—"

That's when I realized something was wrong.

They turned to stare at me, all of 'em together, like they was one person, really. Peeking out from underneath those black hoods was some of the orangest skin I'd ever seen, like they was pumpkins or something. They had weird black eyes and no real noses. Their lips were thin and chins were long and pointed, with warts, like what a witch would wear.

Course I didn't scream or nothing. Didn't know what they were, had never seen nothing like them before, but they was obviously from out of town.

Wouldn't know real prices for anything, and it weren't like we had anything written down, even if they could read.

And maybe they'd be good tippers, besides.

———

I got 'em settled at a table in the center of the saloon. I cut Dusky off, sent him along his way. The businessmen didn't look too happy about the outsiders there, so it weren't too long before they was gone too.

Which left just me and the four newcomers.

"So what'll it be, boys?" I asked, coming out from behind the bar, letting my hips sway just a bit.

None of them paid any attention. They all looked me directly in the face.

That'd never happened before.

"Whissskey," said the first guy. He was a little taller than the others.

I couldn't really read his expression, but he seemed proud of himself.

"Whisky all around?" I asked. They didn't nod, but they didn't disagree either. "I'll bring a bottle. That'll be a quarter eagle." I wasn't about to bring nobody no booze without payment first. At their blank looks, I added "Two-fifty."

It was only two bits more than the regular price. I was just including my tip in the cost.

They had some kind of hissing language they used with each other. Sounded like drunk Mexican to me. The tall one brought out a gold piece from his sleeve and slid it across the table.

I didn't try to count how many fingers he had—as long as he kept them to himself, we was gonna be just fine.

He'd passed me a full eagle—ten whole dollars. "I'll keep this as your tab," I told him, picking up the coin and weighing it. Didn't bother tasting it until after I'd turned away, but it was pure gold as far as I could tell.

I wouldn't have kept the whole thing, if they hadn't spent it all by the end of the evening. I would have given them change. Or at least some of it. My mama may not have been kind, but she did raise me to be fair. Mostly.

I brought 'em back a bottle of the cheapest stuff we had, along with four clean glasses. Then I went back behind the bar, cleaned up Dusky's glass, the businessmen's, and watched my new guests.

They didn't seem quite sure what to do at first. Eventually, they figured it out, pouring the booze into the glasses, then the glasses down their throats.

Maybe they weren't complete strangers, because they swallowed down stuff that would strip the finish off the bar and didn't cough or sputter once.

After they'd finished off a third of the bottle, they seemed to loosen up, as all men do. They leaned back in their chairs, and the tall one even flipped his hood back.

Damn, he was ugly. Bald as a baby's butt, with a dark

web of lines growing like tree roots out of the back of his neck and up into his skull. His black eyes shone wet and long, kind of like a horse's. He hissed at the others, getting them to flip their hoods back too.

The others were just as ugly, though I'd been right— Big Baldy was the tallest of the group, and had the strongest features. The others were smaller, not like kids, but not fully grown, either.

I couldn't make heads or tails outta their hissing talk. They did seem worried about something. I sure hoped it wasn't the money, that they weren't thinking about robbing the place. I couldn't get the day's take out of the bar and to the bank until morning.

While they was pouring another round for themselves, I got the revolver Mister Thomas had given me, that I'd taught all the other girls to use. It weren't one of his inventions, no, it was a real Smith and Wesson, a six-shooter, that I made damn sure was kept cleaner than brand new sheets from the Sears and Roebuck Catalog.

I also started up the coals under the big kettle, so I'd have plenty of steam later if I needed it. Mister Thomas didn't approve of us wasting his special coal and heating up the water before a client asked for a drink from the machine, but I had a feeling about these four.

Once Big Baldy and the others had finished their whisky, I came out from behind the bar again. "Want another?" I asked. They was all leaning way back in their chairs now, loose in the way a cowpoke gets after a hard night's whoring.

"Thisss machine," Big Baldy said, waving his hand toward the beast on the bar. "How much for it?"

"Y'all got enough on your tab for more drinks," I told

him. "Anything special you want? Or should I just make you something?"

"Make ussss, yessss, make usss ssssomething." Big Baldy pressed his thin lips together, tightly, pushing them outward.

Hell, was that a smile? Or was he making a kissy face at me?

I sure didn't stick around to find out. I went back behind the bar, tightened the ends of the hoses connected to the kettle, then opened up the valves so the steam would rise, powering the machine.

It came to life slowly, despite the head of steam I'd already built up. The bottles gurgled—the blue one especially—as seals formed, making sure nothing leaked. Then the dials started lighting up, one after another, showing temperature, pressure, moisture, and a bunch of things Mister Thomas had told me that I didn't remember and couldn't read, having never learned my letters.

So what would it be for Big Baldy? I paused in my considering, looking over the machine at him. He still leaned back, like a lazy cat, playing with the glass in front of him.

What would make him relax more? I remembered thinking about whoring. Maybe that was what this crew needed. Something that would both relax 'em, and raise 'em up.

I started with the yellow—liquid gold, as Mister Thomas likened it. Then some brown: Those boys needed some earthiness. A touch of blue for whimsy. Then topped it off with the pink, for the frills of the dancing girls up the street.

It didn't take the machine long to process, huffing and

puffing as it blended the liquids in its sleek innards, finally distilling the prettiest orange drink at the other end.

I was congratulating myself as I took the first glass over. It looked a perfect match. I was sure to get a big tip from this.

But Big Baldy looked askance at it. "What isss thisss?"

"You asked me to make you something," I shot back.

Mister Thomas would be so mad at me if I wasted a drink from the machine. He sometimes got angry enough to take it out of my wages. I always made it back, though, fixing something that broke either at the bar or in town.

"Ssssomething humansss, yessss," Big Baldy replied.

Human? Well, hell. These boys really weren't from around these parts.

Not like I was gonna stop making 'em drinks, though. We even served Indians here at the Gold Mine Saloon.

"Tis human," I told him. "I made it from the machine built by Mister Thomas. You should try it," I coaxed. "Just a sip. I'm sure it's good for what ails you."

Big Baldy glared at me, glared at the glass I offered him, but he finally reached out with those too-many fingers and took the drink.

He brought it to his nose—no idea if he could smell anything through those tiny slits. I was afraid he was gonna unfurl a tongue or something to taste it first, but he brought it to his mouth, taking a small sip.

After Big Baldy smacked his lips together like an old timer who'd lost all his teeth, he finally looked back up at me. "Issss good!"

"One for each?" I asked, nodding at the other gents.

"Yessss! One for everyone here! You too!" Big Baldy said expansively. "Tell ussss your name?"

"Gracie," I told him. It wouldn't harm none, and might keep 'em friendlier, later.

'Cause I could see that keeping 'em friendly now weren't gonna be a problem—that drink had turned Big Baldy into one jovial pumpkin.

"Now boys, I'm sorry to tell you, but it's closing time," I eventually told Big Baldy and his friends, Frick, Frack, and Nod. I had no idea what any of their names were, but I was plum tired, through and through.

And my feet were *still* killing me.

They'd tossed me an extra eagle, for my troubles. But it weren't enough to keep me going, not when dawn was creeping up outa the east.

"Gracccie," Big Baldy sang out. "Jusssst one more. Pleassssse?"

I'd already planned on that. "Last call," I said. "Last one. Then, vamoose."

Big Baldy actually giggled at that, like a weird pumpkin child. "Vamooooshhhh!" he said, his hand flying through the air, toward Frick, Frack, and Nod.

They chittered at that, like not quite full-grown giggles.

I knew what I should make them to get them moving along—a drink of home.

It was a gamble. It might make 'em morose. I'd done that once already, mixing 'em a drink with too much of the yellow and not enough brown.

But they still needed to be moseying along.

So I gave them great brown muddy skies, with dots of yellow stars, blue hard rocks and soft pink nests.

Then I mixed up something for me. Started with a solid moonshine base, then mixed in a dash of all the colored liquids.

Mister Thomas had told me once never to add everything in. It would muddy the drink. Too much of everything and not enough of a single taste, a single feeling.

But I wasn't so tired that I couldn't coax that machine to sit up and sing for its supper if I set my mind to it.

The drinks for Big Baldy were all a muddy brown, while mine was the color of fire, red and furious.

I'd actually made this drink one time before, named it after myself: Gracie's Fire.

I merely sipped my cordial, planning to finish it later, while the boys slammed theirs back, as I thought they might. "So it's a good evening to ya," I said as I came back out from behind the bar, tray in hand. I collected their glasses and the empty bottle, then turned back toward the bar.

Big Baldy and the others hissed at each other. I had no idea what language it was, but they sounded more intent now, not so relaxed.

I got myself back behind the bar again, brought the revolver up beside me, and waited.

"Gracccccie," Big Baldy said, standing, swaying.

I took a sip of my own drink, "It's been fun, gentlemen, but I gotta close up, and you have to go."

"Not without you, Graccccie," Big Baldy said.

He made that kissy face again. Shit, he was ugly.

"And your marveloussssss massssshine."

Damn it. I knew they was gonna be trouble sooner or later.

I picked up the revolver and cocked it. "Can't have it. Need y'all to just move along, now."

"Gracccccie, you wouldn't ssssshoot usssss," Big Baldy said confidently.

I put a bullet into the floor, directly in front of his feet.

Mama may not have been the best, but she made sure I was well-versed in the essentials: Shooting and moonshine.

Mister Thomas would just have to understand about the hole in the floor.

Big Baldy started, then stood up straight. The others chittered at him. He raised one of his odd, too-many-fingered hands and silenced them.

"I got five bullets still warm and waiting," I told him. "Now, you've been good customers, so let's just leave it at that."

Big Baldy shook his head. "I'm sssssssorry, Gracccccie." He held up some kind of weapon of his own. It looked like a short rifle, but the end was blown out, like a trumpeter's horn.

Now, I'd seen duels out on the street. No one was ever a winner. And while I was fast, I couldn't take down four of them, not before I got myself shot.

I was just gonna have to sweet talk my way out of this. Unfortunately, being sweet wasn't something Mama had ever bothered to teach me.

I kept the gun pointed directly at Big Baldy's chest, while with my other hand I took a sip of my drink. Casual like. Not because I needed the extra courage. Or to prove to myself that I could do this without my hand shaking.

It warmed me from tip to toes, like the sun was already coming up and heating me up on the inside.

"Now, gentlemen," I said. "Let's be reasonable about this. I'm sure we can work something out."

Before I could say another word, Big Baldy shook his head. "No," he said.

Then he shot me.

You know those old houses, out on the prairie, that get abandoned after the fever runs through, or maybe the Indians come in and kill everyone? The way the walls all crumble in, bricks and boards collapsing to dust?

That was how my bones felt. Big Baldy's gun shot out a huge black net that wrapped around my chest, pinning my arms to my sides and making my bones feel like they was all crumbly, nothing solid left inside.

Luckily, I was able to stay upright. Damn boots hurt too much for me to lose feeling with my feet: They was strapped in too tight to turn to dust like the rest of my bones.

Frick, Frack, and Nod all swarmed up over the bar. They made hissing noises at the machine, stroking it and chittering.

Big Baldy looked all too pleased with himself.

But they hadn't pinned my arms all the way, just across my shoulders and my chest. I still had my hands free.

They wasn't paying me no mind.

I didn't have my gun anymore. I'd dropped that when I'd been hit.

But I could still reach my drink.

It was mostly colored moonshine, something these idiots had no idea about.

Mister Thomas could always replace the bar. But he couldn't replace the machine. He'd told me that himself.

With careful, slow movements, I reached for my glass. My hands were shakier than the legs on a newborn calf. I had to watch my fingers to make sure they closed, then tightened, around the drink.

Just as slowly, I brought my hand up and my mouth down, getting a good mouthful of the liquid.

Gracie's Fire.

I didn't swallow it down, though it burned. I took small breaths, afraid the fumes would knock me out.

I took one stumbling step, then another, before I finally reached the lamp on the edge of the bar.

"Gracccccie, where are you going?" Big Baldy asked. He sounded like he was laughing.

That just made me push my poor, abused feet forward one more step. Then another.

I stumbled around the end of the bar until the lamp stood between me and Big Baldy, then clumsily knocked the lamp off, exposing the flame.

"I won't hurtsssss you," Big Baldy assured me.

With my mouth full, I couldn't tell him, *Too bad. Cause I'm about to hurt you.*

Then I blew that pure moonshine straight onto the flame.

An arc of fire jumped from the light and hit Baldy straight in the chest.

Big Baldy fell back on his ass, screaming, his cloak flaming up nicely. He beat at the flames with both hands, not paying me any mind.

Frick, Frack, and Nod took one look at him, and skedaddled.

Seemed they didn't feel like being toasted.

As best I could, I stripped off that damn net. It was sticky and clung to my fingers like spiderwebs. But I peeled it off and dove for my gun, finally holding it with still weak hands, pointing it right at Big Baldy's chest as he rose up from the ground.

The gun he'd used on me was out of his reach, still on the bar. I picked it up too, pointing it straight at his head. "Keeping this as collateral," I told him. "Now git." I started walking toward him.

Big Baldy's cloak was in tatters. Seemed he was just as orange all over, with weird black lines pulsing over his skin, like a map of a river delta.

"We needsssss the massssshine," Big Baldy complained as he started backing toward the door.

"Then come during business hours and make a deal with Mister Thomas," I told him.

When Baldy stopped moving, I put another bullet in the floor. "Git."

"We will return," he warned, but he left.

I locked the doors behind him and leaned back, taking a deep breath.

I had no doubt they'd come back. But I also had faith in Mister Thomas. Once he'd taken apart that gun they'd left behind, he'd know exactly what kind of drink I should serve 'em next time.

I took another sip of Gracie's Fire, thanking Mama for having raised me right, with a steady hand and a solid appreciation of moonshine.

After I made sure that Frick, Frack, and Nod hadn't broken that damn contraption, I could finally close up the saloon for the night, head back up to my garret.

And take my damn boots off.

AUTHOR'S NOTES

I wrote this for an anthology call. It was the first time I'd really written anything steampunk/Wild West.

I really liked Gracie. A lot. I ended up writing half a dozen stories about her, all collected in *The Gracie Stories*.

I have always had plans for more Gracie stories, in particular, one of her traveling across the country by train (and supposedly killing her husband) as well as the story that would follow that one, when Gracie was older and her husband makes a remarkable recovery and returns to her. Don't know if I'll ever get to those, but I may, some day.

THE CURIOUS CASE OF RABBIT AND THE TEMPLE GODDESS

I was late. Again.

And though I knew Master Wei was waiting for me, as impatient as ever, and the gate tower had just sounded the mid-morning hour of the Snake, I still ducked out of the bright spring sunshine and into the temple at the corner of the market.

Familiar peace descended on me in the darkened space. The sounds of the market just beyond the walls faded.

Nine mystical candles stood lit on the rustic wooden altar against the far wall. They were carved with ancient symbols, and circled the tiny silver statue of our beautiful local goddess, Bái Hua Bàn.

I was glad to see that someone had lit them: since the priest had died the month before (and Xin Chao still claimed under mysterious circumstances, not just bad luck) the candles weren't always lit, the rough brick floor not swept, and dogs allowed to foul the temple. The search for the deed to the land the temple sat on hadn't shown up either, more bad luck.

However, my goddess stood, poised as ever, a mysterious smile lurking at the corners of her mouth. Her wide eyes and broad brow showed great intelligence. She stood in flowing robes, offering a simple blossom with both hands to her devotees, a symbol of her purity and great fecundity.

Bái Hua Bàn brought rains to the surrounding fields, children to brighten our days, and wisdom to the elders who guided us. We would be nothing without her, just a speck on the Emperor's maps, a footnote by the census takers, about how this town had once been at this place, and now was no more.

I took a moment to breathe in the stillness, to fortify

myself with the goddess' calm before returning to my hectic day. Some called the temple insignificant. It was only large enough for two dozen standing followers at best. I called it cozy, and comfortable, and in many ways, mine. Though I wasn't a priest, I still attended her, every day, more faithful than a husband.

After my eyes adjusted, I slowly made my way forward over the rough floor—I'd stubbed more than one toe, and broken more than one sandal strap, when I'd used haste. No pews impeded my way: they'd all been shoved to the sides.

I was aware that it was ironic, that someone named *Tù*, or Rabbit, would be so clumsy, and always move slowly. And it was just Rabbit—not Young Rabbit or Old Rabbit, not Fat, Thin, or Spry Rabbit. Not even Number Three or Number Ten Rabbit. Just plain Rabbit, a fitting enough name for an unlucky fourth son of a now-widowed mother, the only one still unmarried and living at home.

When I was close enough to smell the lilies on the edge of the altar, I realized someone else shared my haven. He was prostrate on the floor, covered in a dark cloak, a mere shadow.

He hadn't positioned himself in the middle, the Emperor's place, but to the stronger, right-hand side.

I moved to the left side to give him some privacy, though I was curious. I didn't recognize him, and I knew all the goddess' followers. Maybe he was some foreigner and the goddess had spoken to him, calling to him from far away.

I bowed to the corners of the world, starting with the west, where the sacred Emperor and his golden court reigned, then to the north, where the horse barbarians waged endless war, to the east where tales of strange beasts and the ocean lay, finally, to the south where there were yet more barbarians, but at least they were our own.

Then I bowed to the most important point, the center, where the town of Da Shan rose up and spread around me, the heart of my world.

Only then did I kneel and prostrate myself, giving all I had to my goddess.

I've had scholars argue with me at Tang's Tea Shop, claiming that she's just a local goddess, here, at the southern end of Da Shan. That I shouldn't pay her so much attention, she couldn't be that important.

I told them I didn't care what other gods or goddesses existed elsewhere, even at the north end of the town. She was important to me.

Bái Huā Bàn was who I poured my heart out to, who I entrusted with my secrets. I told her of my upcoming day, the trials of being merely a clerk, not even an apprentice, of my cramped, ink-stained fingers, my caged soul that longed for poetry but was enslaved to writing contracts.

She never replied. I didn't expect her to. Not really. I was just a lowly clerk.

Still. I visited her every day, and since the priest had died, more often than that.

I kept my thanks and ramblings short that morning, asking her for blessings for myself, my mother, my master, my town, and my emperor.

When I raised my head, I wondered briefly if a storm had suddenly gathered. The temple was no longer as brightly lit.

Had some of the candles blown out?

It took me another long heartbeat to realize that the nine candles burned around an empty spot.

The statue of the goddess was gone.

As was the shadow man.

Trembling, I stood, unsure what to do.

Fat Ang, the local magistrate, wouldn't believe any tales of a shadow man. He would send his bullies to pick up whoever he thought needed a lesson.

Or he might accuse me of such a crime. I *was* always here.

No one would search for the real thief.

I moved closer.

A single petal from a white lotus flower marked the spot where my perfect Bái Hua Bàn had stood.

Before I could gather up this precious artifact, the edges of it started to brown. As I watched, lines of age shot through the creamy flesh, withering the petal, as if a hidden winter hand had scraped its poisonous fingernail along it. It finally shriveled up completely and disappeared.

The message was clear.

I must find the statue, and return it, or all the bad luck Bái Hua Bàn constantly held back would descend. It would be worse than any plague or famine: My town would be no more.

I rushed through the crooked back streets, fast enough that no devil could follow me.

I had to think. I had to plan.

Who was that shadow? Why would he take the statue of Bái Hua Bàn?

Though I loved her with all my heart, I had long suspected the statue itself to be only silver-plated. The thief would make more by robbing the ancient tea shops that lay outside the town, next to the kilns and just before the graveyard, that only desperate men and loose women frequented.

So if the shadow man didn't melt it down, and he couldn't sell it, not easily, not anywhere local, why had he taken it? What did he plan to do with it?

And why had the goddess placed this burden on me?

I fretted, wringing my hands as I hurried along, finally ducking into the narrow alley between the two weaver's shops, barely wide enough for a thin man, stumbling into the brightness of the far courtyard. The acrid smell of dye slammed into me, causing my eyes to tear up, making me nearly trip and fall into the huge vat of orange dye set up just at the entrance.

I hurried past the good natured cursing of Master Yen, the head weaver, and scurried up the creaky wooden stairs that led to my office.

Though really, calling it an office was to give it grandeur. In reality, it was a cramped room that froze in the winter and boiled in the summer, stacked floor to ceiling with molding, moth-eaten, scrolls and folding books. Two desks were moored in the center of it, with books piled in shoals around them. Papers and more books covered the desks, and if I wasn't diligent, would impede the path from the door, as well as the two, hard, cushion-less stools that we sat on.

We were the dirty secret of the local *Xi* office, as well as more than one law office: most of the contracts involving land sales and wills were sent to us to compose and record. I don't know what the *Xi* clerks did in their official capacity, besides hold poetry contests and challenge each other to create the most fanciful meals.

Master Wei was already there, wearing his standard gray linen robes, hovering like a stained ghost. He started grumbling as soon as he saw me.

"Lazy boy! Where have you been? Do you think these contracts will write themselves? That those deeds will copy themselves over? Do you know how many *bao* coin you cost me every time you're late?"

I bowed almost in half to address him.

"Master, please, listen to me. I have something to tell you."

But Master Wei continued. "I don't know why I keep paying you, given how you steal from me. It was a favor, a debt, *guanxie*, for your dear departed father. But—"

"Please! Master Wei! Something happened!"

I raised my head from my still folded over position.

Master Wei's pinched face and turned down mouth gathered tighter together. His perpetually squinting eyes blinked rapidly.

"Well? Go on. If you're going to interrupt your elders, you should at least say something."

"The status of Bái Hua Bàn, in the market temple, was taken!"

"So?" Master Wei asked, still blinking rapidly.

I stood up, my mouth agape.

He gave a loud *hrmph*. "I'm surprised it wasn't stolen years ago and melted down. You can't trust the people in this town anymore. Particularly the young people. When I was a boy—"

"I'm sorry, master. I know your stories are always educational. But what about the statue? What should we do?"

Master Wei *hrmphed* again.

"You should stop wringing your hands like an old woman," he said brusquely.

I forced myself to unbend my arms and leave my hands still by my sides.

"And *we* can do nothing."

"Nothing?" I asked.

I might have squeaked.

"This is temple business."

"But the priest—"

"Is dead. I know. Unlucky business. And the deed to the temple land lost." Master Wei gave a dramatic shudder. "And now you have work to do."

I knew there would be no arguing with him, not at that time, so I shuffled dutifully to my desk and began my preparations for the day. I tied back the sleeves of my plain gray robe. Mother had already replaced the cuffs with colorful plackets three times to hide the stains.

The way my day had gone, she'd have to do it a fourth time, soon.

Thus prepared, I picked up the first scroll. It had originated from Jing and Sons. I silenced my groan. The clerk there was barely literate and had no sense of style. The writing was in a cramped hand, the characters staggering across the page like drunken ants.

I had only finished recopying the third line when the squeaking of the rickety stairs warned me that someone was coming up. I put on my earnest face, the one Master Wei made me practice, saying we wanted to sell our services, not look constipated.

However, it wasn't an important client. Instead, it was Fat Ang, the local magistrate, and two of his bullies.

He'd been charged by the local governor to keep the peace. He always acted as if his district was one of the

Hundred Li provinces, instead of merely a Hundred Families town.

He'd failed all three attempts at taking the local civic exams, doing so badly at deportment that not even bribes could help him. He still wore the orange robes of the lowest level government official. It split at the seams around his grossly overweight body.

Both Master Wei and I rose as they came in the door. I'm sure my master rose to offer the potential clients beverages, while I—I must admit—I rose in fear.

At least I remembered to keep my hands firmly clasped in front of me and not wring them.

Fat Ang stood just inside the doorway, his beady eyes darting greedily from the scrolls to the desks to my master's fine writing brushes. He stood with his hands behind his back, evidence of his breakfast still spilled down the front of his robe. His neck was short and squat, like a foreign wrestler's, his head melted onto his shoulders.

"Ah, gentlemen," Master Wei said graciously, using his second-best customer voice, reserved for rich merchants and lords fallen on hard times. "How might I assist you today?"

Fat Ang grimaced and made a sucking noise, as if to dislodge something stuck in one of the gaping holes between his teeth. Finally, whatever morsel he'd been seeking freed itself and he spoke. "Not you we came to see. Want him," he added, indicating me with his chin.

Before the two bullies could further desecrate our work abode, Master Wei came out from behind his desk and confronted them.

I'd never noticed before how tall Master Wei was. He was always stopped over, muttering about contracts and wasted coin. At his full height, he easily stood a head above Fat Ang, his gray whiskers lending him an air of wisdom, though his dark eyes still squinted under his bushy white brows.

"Why? What has my impudent apprentice done now?" Master Wei thundered.

I opened my mouth to correct him, then closed it again.

Apprentice? We'd never had such a relationship formalized. I was no heir to him, not training for anything better, merely a clerk, another, and according to him, totally inadequate pair of hands to merely copy contracts I could never hope to understand.

By declaring me his apprentice, he took responsibility for me.

If the magistrate decided to arrest me, well, he might have cause to arrest Master Wei too.

"The statue of Bái Hua Bàn is missing," Fat Ang replied after sucking at his teeth again. "That one," he said, rudely pointing directly at me this time, "Was the last one seen leaving the temple. Hurrying away, like he was worried."

"Of course he was worried," Master Wei scoffed. "He was late attending his duties to me."

He threw a glare at me over his shoulder.

I tried to look properly chastised, but really, who had expected such a performance from my old master?

"I don't know," Fat Ang said, rocking back on his heels. "He's always sneaking into that temple, then sneaking out again. He mighta been lookin' to steal it the whole time."

Master Wei drew himself up to frostier heights. "Are you saying that this establishment would stoop to hiring thieves now? Would you slander not only me, but my business?"

"Now, now," Fat Ang said, holding out his hands to try to placate Master Wei. "I'm just sayin' he has an attitude to him. Sneaky like."

Master Wei sighed and shook his head. "I ask you. Really. Does he even *look* intelligent enough to have pulled off a crime such as this? Stealing a treasured statue from a temple in broad daylight? On the edge of the market, no less? He wouldn't have managed three steps before he'd have dropped it or something."

I didn't know whether to look outraged or pitiful. From the sneer Fat Ang threw at me, I probably accomplished a little of both.

"I won't bother your 'fine establishment' any longer," Fat Ang said, sarcasm dripping from his words as freely as the sweat sliding down my back. "But we'll be keeping an eye on him. Make sure he don't rabbit off. You get it? Rabbit?" He laughed at his own joke, his two bullies joining in.

"Rabbit. Of course," Master Wei said, dryly.

I could just imagine the glare he was throwing at them, the one that looked like respect but really, if you knew him, you could see it was laced with disgust.

"Now, if you hear anything—"

"You shall be the very first person we think of," Master Wei assured him.

As soon as the magistrate had gone, Master Wei turned to me, his stature shrinking and his eyes hard and angry. "Deceitful toad," he muttered. "Did I ever tell you the time he—never mind."

Master Wei peered at me for a moment, then he went

back to his desk and started shuffling through the contracts on the left, the ones delivered that morning.

Hope flared in me, brighter than the sparklers at the annual Luna celebration. "What are we going to do, then?" I asked, breathless with excitement.

"Do? Do? We're going to do our work," Master Wei said.

He shoved a contract at me without looking.

"Finish what you're doing. And quickly. This is the next one that must be done before any of your regular breaks, or tea time. If you think you can manage that?"

He glanced over his shoulder, a curious cold challenge in his glare.

"I will," I told him, defeated.

Not only did I not have any help finding the real culprit of the theft, it was obvious Fat Ang would accuse me of it the first chance he got.

Plus, my lovely lady was gone, and if I didn't find the statue soon, well, I didn't want to even imagine the bad luck that would befall me.

I sat, crushed.

Maybe once I'd finished these pages, I could make an excuse to go to Tang's Tea Shop. If anyone knew about the other suspects, or had any other clues, Xin Chao, the owner's son, would have heard.

With that in mind, I began to copy in earnest, finishing the first scroll and picking up the new contract Master Wei had handed to me.

I scanned it quickly to get the gist of it. No matter what Master Wei might accuse me of, I *was* fully literate, and rarely had to look up any symbols or characters.

Old Mu, the woodworker whose shop stood next to Bái Hua Bàn's temple had died the month before, about the same time as the priest. I remembered that, and how mourners had sometimes been confused, going to pay their respects to the wrong household. Old Mu had left his house and shop to his son, Nyjiang. Standard enough.

Now, Nyjiang was intent on expanding his shop and purchasing the land adjoining it. Also, fairly standard in these modern times, when merchants had the coin to buy land, as well as the legal standing not only to hold onto it, but to pass it to both sons and daughters.

I started pulling together the standard paragraphs to describe such a sale when it finally dawned on me exactly what land Nyjiang was intending to buy.

The lot south of his.

Where the market temple stood.

I knew the deed to the temple land had been lost, but that didn't mean he could grab it, did he?

I raced for the scrolls on the far wall, that contained the record of all land purchases in the town for the past hundred years.

I quickly learned that the original consortium of owners who had donated money to build the temple and keep it running had feuded, bitterly, at the end of their days. Instead of retaining the title to the land, they'd passed it to the priests of the temple.

But the deed hadn't been found. Nor a will.

I was starting to wonder if Xin Chao had been right, and the priest had died of something other than bad luck.

And maybe Old Mu as well.

"Master!" I exclaimed as I reached the end of my studies.

"Eh," he said casually, as if I'd approached him to ask about dinner, not standing there with wide eyes and trembling hands. "I suppose you think you're entitled to some sort of break now." His hard eyes glittered with secret amusement.

"I—umh—I do," I finally acknowledged.

"You just have to say so," he grumbled. "Ask for what you want. I'm no red-faced, hungry demon."

I stared at him, confused. What was he actually saying?

"Go on, go on," Master Wei said, throwing his hands up as if in despair. "You'll be useless until you get your tea. More useless than usual," he added with a glare.

"Thank you, Master Wei," I told him, giving him a low bow. "Your generosity is overwhelming as always."

"Be sure to bring back a steamed pork bun!" he called out as I hurried through the door, taking my life in my hands as I rushed down the rickety steps.

"I will!" I called back to him as I surged forward, narrowly missing yet another vat of bright dye as I raced across the courtyard.

I had a clue, my first real clue, about Bái Hua Bàn's missing statue.

Now, I just had to figure out what to do next.

Tang's Tea Shop sat in northern part of the market, on the opposite corner of the square from Bái Hua Bàn's temple. I considered passing by the temple, but I spied more of Fat Ang's men in the street just outside, so I rushed directly to the tea shop instead.

The front of the shop lay open to the street, with low tables and cushions in before the shop, at street level, as well as more in the shop. Lamps hung only in the back, over the fires where the water was constantly boiling, making the blackened walls sweat. The rest of the room was dim, covered with murals of pure imagined mountains where tea leaves grew.

Old men stretched out along the stairs, escaping the heat of the shop, having the same arguments they'd been having since they were boys. They nodded to me as I passed by, their eyes accusing me of things I'd never even thought of, as always.

Ling-Ling, Xin Chao's older sister, was doing a high pour at one of the inside tables. She was quite an artist, two tendrils of hair carefully escaping from her tight bun, perfectly framing her delicate face, distracting her victims from her greedy mouth and calculating eyes. Her robe was respectfully draped, but her sleeves were drawn up a bit too high, and cinched a bit too tightly.

She lifted the kettle high above her head and dribbled a stream of water into the pot below, on the table, without splashing a drop. It was always quite a show. I waited until she was finished before catching her eye.

She didn't bother to speak to me—I couldn't provide her with any gifts or coin—she just jerked her head and indicated the back of the shop.

I rushed past the boiling kitchen and through the back hallway to the courtyard behind the building. Two old trees in the middle of the open space cast strong shade, keeping the courtyard cool and pleasant. None of the other shop keepers or their families were out there: then again, they usually were up front, minding the shops, until late in the evening.

Xin Chao was swinging an ax, efficiently decimating a pile of wood into kindling to feed the fires in the front. Long Yen was there as well. He was the son of the head of the Weaver's Guild. He sat at the base of one of the trees, watching Xin Chao, and probably offering completely unnecessary advice.

"So? Did you?" Long Yen asked as soon as he saw me.

"Did I?" I asked, momentarily confused. Then I realized that even my friends were accusing me.

"I'm assuming you mean the statue? No, I didn't take it." I stood glaring at him, fists pressed into my waist.

Long Yen often made even a shy rabbit like me want to strangle him.

He grinned up at me, loose and easy as always. He wore the finest dyed red robes, rich and well made.

Xin Chao stopped chopping and stood resting against his ax. The smell of fresh cut wood overlaid the scent of burnt tea. He had tied his hair back with a green rag, looking like a sailor from a street performance. His dark gray linen robes and trousers hid his sweat, though his face was shining with it.

He looked like a strong ox, happy and content with his world, though he worked harder than Long Yen and I combined.

I knew even trying to swing his ax would have me toppling over.

Then again, his mother had to keep the accounts and ledger—he claimed that the numbers and letters grew legs and danced around the page when he tried to view them.

"So, you didn't take it. Good for you. Who did?" Long Yen asked.

"What do the old men say?" I asked, jerking my head and indicating the front of the store.

"You, of course, top their lists," Xin Chao said with a grin. "Though at least half think you're not bright enough to have done it."

I groaned. Wonderful. Either I was a thief or incompetent.

"Anyone else?"

Long Yen rolled his eyes. "Foreign devils, of course. The priests from the northern temple. But I bet you know something, don't you?"

"How about Nyjiang?"

For the first time, Long Yen dropped his constant mask of *ennui* and looked interested. "That's a new name. Why him?"

"He's applied to purchase the land the temple sits on," I told them in a rush. "Since the land's in dispute, he may be able to grab it. Plus, if the statue's gone..."

"Clever," Long Yen said.

"But there's no proof," I told them, squatting down, the reality of the situation crashing down on me again.

"Then get the proof," Xin Chao said, shouldering his ax. "Maybe he snuck over there early this morning. Maybe someone saw him."

I opened my mouth, then shut it again. I glanced around the courtyard, though of course, no one was there but the three of us.

I leaned in closer. Long Yen and Xin Chao also leaned in.

"I saw who took the statue," I confessed.

"Did you tell the magistrate?" Xin Chao asked.

"I couldn't. He was just a shadow—one moment prostrate on the floor, the next, gone. And so was the statue."

"Foreign devil, then," Long Yen proclaimed.

"I can't prove it. And Fat Ang, like everyone else," I added with a glare at both of them, "already thinks I stole it."

"Then you'll just have to prove you didn't take it," Xin Chao said reasonably.

"But I didn't take it!" I protested, standing and pacing.

"You know, there is a way you can prove it," Long Yen said, leaning back again and taking a long drink of tea.

From his smirk, I knew I wasn't going to like this.

I asked anyway.

"How?"

"By stealing it back."

"This is a bad idea," I said yet again as I crouched in the alley behind Nyjiang's woodshop.

While the smell of freshly cut wood at Tang's Tea Shop had filled me with the idea of success after labor, now, here, it smelled like butchered hope.

Long Yen, crouched behind me, merely laid a hand on my shoulder. "Shh," he whispered. "And stop wringing your hands."

I forced my hands to my sides, but I couldn't stop their trembling. The few meager mouthfuls of soup that I'd managed at dinner threatened to erupt from my stomach. I was sweating, worse than when I'd seen Fat Ang that morning.

How had my supposed friends talked me into breaking into Nyjiang's woodshop?

"Look. See!" Xin Chao whispered urgently from his place in front of me. "Nyjiang has finally sent everyone home for the night!"

I shivered in anticipation—of either the deed or the inevitable consequence of getting caught, I wasn't sure.

Gnats swarmed just above us, a good reminder to stay

low and take shallow breaths. I dreaded swallowing one and giving us away with my hacking.

We crept a few steps closer, peering through the slats of Nyjiang's back fence.

Lamps in the front of the shop had long since been blown out. Now a single globe remained, illuminating Nyjiang.

He sat whittling a small whistle, a toy for a child. He worked slowly, deliberately, his blade flashing in the night. He wore a plain, forest green robe with a heavy leather apron over it. His hair was cut shorter than was fashionable, and though he wasn't much older than I, he was already balding at the crown, a sure sign he'd been plotting too much. His face was thin and pinched, his lips pursed, as if he were about to whistle himself.

As the gate tower bells sounded the late evening hour of the Dog, a shadow flowed out of the corner of the yard.

How long had he been there? Had he seen us? Heard us?

I stood to run away.

Both Long Yen and Xin Chao were ready and pulled me back down. I silently swatted at the gnats that had settled on my neck and threatened to crawl into my ears, missing Nyjiang's greeting of the shadow man.

A husky laugh drew my attention. The mystery man spoke. "No, no tea. Or pickled young carrots or rice crackers. Business is all I'm here for."

"Very well." Nyjiang drove the point of his knife into the table with a solid *thunk*. It stood as a barrier between them, Nyjiang standing on his side, dark and brooding, while the other man was still just a shadow in black robes, his hood drawn up, hiding his features.

His accent placed him from south of here, how far

south, I couldn't say. But he wasn't a local, and he wasn't a foreigner either.

"Do you have it?" Nyjiang asked.

From a fold in his cloak, the shadow man brought out the shining statue of Bái Hua Bàn.

I couldn't take my eyes from it. Even in his profane hands, it shone with a pure, sacred light.

Suddenly, I knew we were doing the right thing. The statue called to me, needing me. I knew it was just my poetic soul taking flight, however, I still heard it. I wanted to jump the fence, quick as a rabbit, and steal her back right then, but I controlled myself.

Nyjiang produced a leather purse and threw it on the table.

Even I recognized the clink of many coins.

"Aren't you going to count it?" Nyjiang asked as the shadow man turned to go.

"I know where you sleep," the man said simply, the threat clear.

I shivered again. Nyjiang certainly had hired someone better than he'd realized.

The shadow disappeared into the night. I felt the fence move slightly under my palm—I assumed he'd flowed over it and departed.

Nyjiang, in the meanwhile, lit more candles. He examined the statue from every angle.

I nearly growled at his mishandling of the goddess' image.

Finally, Nyjiang loosened his knife from the table and pried off the bottom of the base. He shook the statue, hard, as if trying to loosen something inside of it.

Nothing came out.

Cursing, Nyjiang brought the lights closer. He got a chopstick and used it to probe inside the statue.

I felt a little sick at how badly he was mistreating Bái Hua Bàn.

However, whatever he was expecting to find wasn't there. After a bit, he reassembled the base and put the statue on the table. He sat, head bowed, almost like a man in prayer.

My hope rose—was he going to do the right thing? And replace the statue?

I wanted to weep when he brought a cheap burlap sack from inside the store and tossed the statue into it.

I was going to make him pay for his degradation of Her.

He got a shovel and dug a quick hole, placing her carelessly in it, then covering her up, blowing out the candles and heading upstairs to his bed.

He would pay ten thousand times, I swore.

I was the first one over the fence, digging madly at the dirt, as if I had to rescue a living, breathing being from drowning in the dirt.

Long Yen pulled me to the side and Xin Chao made quick work of the hole.

Then, finally, the statue was back out in the open. I trembled to be holding her so closely. She was even more perfect than I remembered.

I might have cried a tear or two.

My friends got me back over the wall.

"Do we take her back to the temple now? Or wait until sunrise?" Xin Chao asked.

"What about Nyjiang?" I said. He had to pay.

"He doesn't matter," Long Yen whispered. "It will be a miracle. The goddess' temple will be saved."

"Until Nyjiang steals her again," I muttered, clutching the statue against my chest.

I knew I didn't want to let her go for personal reasons —it was amazing to hold her like this—but I also didn't think she was safe.

"True," a silky voice came out of the darkness.

Suddenly, the shadow man was in front of us.

"I will just steal her again."

"The statue belongs in the temple," I hissed at the shadow man, proud of how my voice didn't tremble at all.

I hoped the night and the darkness hid how my hands shook. At least Long Yen and Xin Chao still stood beside me as we confronted the thief in the alley behind Nyjiang's shop.

"No, the statue belongs with me."

The shadow man stepped closer. The long silver point of his blade shone in what little light there was.

I gulped, but didn't stand down. "The goddess will shower Da Shan with bad luck if I don't return her image." Then I bravely added, "And I wouldn't want to be in your sandals, either."

"How much more havoc do you think your goddess will cause if her temple is torn down?"

"Her temple is going to remain just where it is," I told him. "Housing her image."

The shadow man laughed.

Chicken flesh raised all across my shoulders. How could a laugh be more threatening than the cold blade he wielded?

"Don't you want to know what Nyjiang was actually after?" he taunted.

In his other hand, a small scroll appeared.

"The deed to the temple land," he promised. "And the priest's will."

"The priest had hidden it inside the statue?" Long Yen asked.

It made sense to me. No one would steal it. No one local would dare.

Only someone like our shadow man.

I glanced at my friends. There were three of us. Couldn't we just take the scroll from him? Xin Chao was strong, and Long Yen was clever and sly.

The fight may bring the guard, though, and they'd never listen to my excuses: they'd just accuse me of being the thief, since I was holding the statue.

The point of the blade was suddenly very close to my neck.

"Now, while I may be a thief, I do have principles," he said, sliding closer. "I have a patron who will pay dearly for this kind of crude, local art."

"What?"

I must admit, I did squawk.

"However, this paper is useless to me." He waved it as negligently as one of Xin Chao's older sisters wielded her fan. "I offer it to you in trade."

"And?" I asked, surprised to hear the steel in my voice.

He had all the power, all the luck. What was he really asking for?

"You are a clever one for such a timid rabbit," the shadow man said. "And a future favor."

"But—" I sputtered.

"It will be legal. Well. Mostly legal," he assured me.

I didn't want to promise this man anything. Particularly not in front of witnesses.

But all of Da Shan, perhaps even all the Middle Kingdom, worked on debts and *guanxie*.

So in the dark of the night, under the threat of impalement, I exchanged my lovely goddess' image for her continued existence.

"Don't worry, I'll take the best care of her," the shadow man assured me before he disappeared.

I could only hope I'd receive the same sort of treatment from her.

Kan Ou, the priest's heir, sat in the chair reserved for the most prestigious clients, next to Master Wei's desk. He wore his thick hair long, around his broad shoulders, framing his frankly perfect face. He was the third son of a farmer who lived a couple of *li* outside of town.

I had rarely seen him at the temple: his habit had been to walk into Da Shan every morning before the sun rose, sing hymns in pure, clear tones with the priest, then walk back to tend to his father's fields. He had the constant expression of a moon-struck calf and was more devout than I.

I hated him on sight.

However, the *Xi* offices had recognized him as the new priest, acknowledging his claim to the temple land. Master Wei had found him, and we had provided him with a copy of the will and the deed.

When Master Wei introduced us at the end of Kan Ou's visit, his liquid eyes grew wider when he heard my name.

"The priest talked of you all the time. He said if I didn't want the temple, he would deed it to you. Do you want it?"

The boy's offer was sincere, as pure as his heart.

I looked over his head at Master Wei, whose attention was suddenly drawn by the papers on his desk.

Before all this, I would have agreed in a heartbeat. I hated the contracts and the law, my crabbed fingers, the musty office.

But Master Wei had called me an apprentice, claimed me as his own.

I knew I owed him. It was my *guanxie* to stay.

"No, my duty is here, while yours is to our goddess."

"Thank you for allowing me to follow my dream."

Kan Ou rose from his seat, then bent in half, bowing low to me.

"Just take care of her," I growled at him.

I sounded like Master Wei.

"I will. I will. I have already enough donations to commission a new statue. Would you like to donate?"

He turned those innocent, expectant eyes on me.

I couldn't resist any more than the clerks at the *Xi* office, who had probably already filled his purse.

After Kan Ou left, I went back to my desk. My hand trembled, but I still picked up the papers there, then I made myself walk back to Master Wei's desk and hand the papers to him.

"What are these?" he asked, squinting over the top of them at me.

I kept my hands still at my sides, my voice calm and steady. "Apprenticeship papers, sir."

"Eh," Master Wei said, sitting down at his crowded

desk. He got out the name chop for his office and a jar of fine red ink.

"About time," he muttered as he stamped the papers, agreeing to my terms.

I should have asked for more.

That evening I went back to Bái Hua Bàn's temple to pray, to thank her for my good luck, to reassure her that she was safe in her place, secure, though I was certain Kan Ou had already told her everything. Nyjiang's application for her land had been denied with the appearance of the temple land deed.

I didn't know what I would do to make Nyjiang pay, but I thought about it frequently. I knew I had time.

No one would suspect the quiet rabbit in the corner of thinking like a snake.

The gap where Bái Hua Bàn's brilliant statue had once stood was filled with sunlight that shone from the tiny window at the back.

I prostrated myself. I prayed and chatted.

After I stood again, I spent some time watching the golden dust motes dance where her statue soon would return.

The air seemed to pause.

For the briefest of moments, I felt the press of something petal soft against my cheek.

Perhaps a single kiss?

Then it was gone, and the afternoon returned to how it had been, the sounds of the market behind me, the dancing sunlight, the scent of rain on the wind.

And I knew that the goddess was pleased, that I had done well, and that this plain, simple rabbit had grown.

AUTHOR'S NOTES

Like so many of the others, I wrote this story for a workshop. I figured that the teacher would tell me it was awful, that I needed to do so much work on it, etc. It's a mash-up of things: it's silly and light, historic, and all about Chinese land law.

Instead, the instructor told me to fix a couple of typos and send it out.

Alfred Hitchcock Mystery Magazine bought it. As well as subsequent Rabbit stories that I wrote.

All the Rabbit stories are collected together in *The Rabbit Mysteries*. There may or may not be one more Rabbit story someday, about him finding a wife. But I'm also pleased with where I've left him in terms of his character arc.

SISTERS

Lin Han still knelt in the courtyard, as still as the towering rock *stelae* behind her that the names of her family's ancestors were carved into. The bleak early morning light washed everything gray: the hard brick she knelt on, the black iron brazier in front of her, the twisted pine in front of the double wall that stood guard before the door leaving the family courtyard. The sacred smoke from the brazier had long since disappeared, but the heavy smell of burnt wood and paint still hung in the air.

Double-hour bells rang in the distance, muffled by Lin Han's fog. She felt herself stirring, as if she were waking, though she hadn't slept all night. She blinked dry eyes and stiffness poured through her body, as if she were suddenly no longer young. Her knees started to ache. Her shoulders felt weighed down, as if a yoke with buckets filled with water lay across them, like the laborers she saw in the street. She took a deep breath, the taste of smoke mingling with the tears still gathered at the back of her throat.

Lin Han curled her fingers into fists on her thighs, realizing how cold the tops of her hands were when they touched the warm silk. She pushed herself forward, trying to rise, and ended up catching herself with her hands, the cold hard brick pushing back at her. Her legs were filled with sand, leaden, hard to move.

Slowly Lin Han rose. She swayed like young bamboo in a storm trying to gain her feet.

As if that was a signal, Old Cook scurried out.

"Please, Miss, you must go to bed now," he whispered urgently.

"No. I will not leave my sister," Lin Han said.

Old Cook didn't have to say it. She heard it echoing again against the hard bricks of the courtyard, the proclamation by her mother, her father.

You no longer have a sister.

"Enough of that," Lin Han said, banishing those ghosts of memory. "I must take her with me." Sometime in the night a plan had come to her.

Old Cook opened his mouth, then closed it and gestured at the huge brazier. It had *Fu* dog heads on the sides, each bigger than Lin Han's head. Ornate legs curved down to splayed toes. It had taken six men to haul it into the courtyard.

Lin Han had grown the last year, and so it merely came up to her chest now. However, she would never grow big enough to carry it away.

"Fine," she said. "I need, I need…"

The chill of the morning finally entered her bones. She shivered abruptly and swayed again. But she refused to give in to the horror of it, what she needed to do.

"I need something to hold her in."

"Right away, Miss." Old Cook bowed low before racing away.

The long shadows of the courtyard wall to Lin Han's right began defining as the sun rose. The twisted pine took on long needles and distinct branches. The brilliant red tile on the rooftops beyond the courtyard sprang to life. All around the quiet courtyard the city of Yen Tu woke up. Already the street venders with their buckets of millet porridge and clear chicken broth called out their wares. People walked in the street, snatches of conversation floating up over the wall.

Lin Han just waited.

Old Cook came back out with an ornate, porcelain, red-and-white vase. It was skinny at the bottom and blossomed out at the top. Hard nubs of white stuck out from the body in curling lines.

Dao Ming would have wanted to put tall lilies in it, something graceful and overflowing.

Lin Han accepted the weight of the vase, cradling it in her arms for a moment before taking the cold metal scoop that Old Cook also handed her. She stood on her toes and looked into the brazier.

The pile of ash was so small, like Dao Ming had been.

Mama would kill Lin Han for handling ashes. She'd insist on a cleansing ceremony from the stinky Taoist priest with the dark robes who never smiled as well as a second one from the Buddhist priest in his bright orange robes who was more sour still.

Tears gathered behind Lin Han's eyes again. This was all she had left of her younger sister. A burnt spirit tablet, taken from their ancestors' altar in the front greeting room.

A hard spike of hurt pierced her chest as she remembered how her parents were going to deny Dao Ming's birth, just like they'd denied her death. They claimed now that there had only ever been two children: Lin Han and her older brother. Dao Ming had been written out of the family records. Father had talked of bribing the census takers to cross out her name. All her clothes had been given away or burned. Her favorite straw-stuff doll destroyed.

Last night, Mama and Father hadn't even held a funeral, barely said a single prayer before they'd placed Dao Ming's spirit tablet in the brazier.

Someone had to do something for Dao Ming. There was nothing to anchor her spirit. She would become a red-faced angry ghost, stealing food and paper ghost money meant for others.

Lin Han's tears fell as she stuck the shovel in the ashes.

The mound crumbled, the fine ash sliding away like sand. When she lifted the first scoop, the early morning breeze puffed away some of the soot, sending it dancing across the courtyard.

She carefully tipped the scoop into the vase so no more of the ash escaped. Moving slowly, she completed her task, though some of it had spilled onto her fine dark-blue robes. Mama would be mad, but Lin Han didn't care.

Finally, Lin Han stepped back. With a bow, she solemnly handed the small scoop to Old Cook, who just as solemnly took it.

"I will bury this," Old Cook assured her.

Lin Han swallowed around a dry mouth. "Thank you," she whispered, touched that he was treating Dao Ming's burnt spirit tablet like a body, as if they were actually handling the dead.

"You take care of Little Miss," Old Cook instructed. "We will hide you as well as we can today, me and the gardener and your mother's dressing maid."

"Thank you," Lin Han said again, bowing low.

Though her family might deny Dao Ming, Lin Han was still going to see that at least in the afterlife, her sister would be taken care of.

Lin Han stood on one side of the dusty street, looking at the Taoist priest's shop on the other. The tiny wooden shack sat nestled between two larger stone buildings, almost as if he'd blocked off an alley to make his home. No paint decorated the walls, no mystic symbols were carved into the wood. Just a hand painted sign, weathered gray wood with bright red paint promising suitable mates for all.

The mid-morning bells had already rung. A few laborers remained in the street, squatting under the eaves of one of the stone buildings, rolling dice and drinking strong pear wine. They hadn't seemed to notice her—no one had. Lin Han knew her fine blue robes didn't belong in this part of Yen Tu, knew that the vase she carried was worth more than a few *cash*.

Either Dao Ming protected her, or Lin Han had also turned into a ghost.

Finally, the old man she'd watched go into the Taoist's shop came out. He clutched a brown leather bag tightly to his chest as he hurried off. Maybe the old Taoist was also an apothecary, though he didn't have a sign for that.

Feeling great daring, Lin Han stepped out of the shadows and into the brightly lit street. She rushed across though there was no traffic, no people or palanquins to avoid this far from the city center. She fumbled with the latch and had to use her elbow to push on it so she wouldn't have to put down the vase.

The dark of the shop made Lin Han stop and blink her eyes for a moment. Spicy medicine smells, the scent of burnt *jing* sticks and incense all came to her, as well as long boiled tea and sweet chrysanthemum. The Taoist sat silent and still behind the counter against the far wall. Rough wooden floorboards snagged her sandals as she walked forward.

Jars bigger than her vase filled with bulbous white roots in yellow liquid hung from ropes from the ceiling. A long dried snake skin marked with a black diamond pattern stretched from one of the room to the other and swayed in the slightest breeze. Eggs cooked in tea sat in another jar on the counter. The back wall held row after row of sealed porcelain jars, all meticulously labeled with either red or black characters.

The Taoist rose from his seat. His long face ended with a hanging jowl and his forehead lifted up to a bald skull. Fringes of greasy white hair curled down from just above his ears, over his shoulders. His nose hung like a foreigner's and his ears stood out like long handles.

"Good day," he said, giving her a small bow. He voice belied his skeletal stature, ringing from him like a deep bell.

"Good day," Lin Han said. She hugged the vase closer to her, the hard nubs pressing into her chest. "I need to find a mate."

At his raised eyebrow, she made her voice stronger. "For my sister."

She carefully lifted the vase out to show him, missing its hard pressure against her chest. "The ashes...the ashes of her spirit tablet are in here."

"Ah, a *minghu*," the Taoist priest said, nodding. "A spirit wedding."

"You must find someone who will look after her. She was, she was a good girl. She will work hard. But she should also be respected. Honored."

"Thank you for honoring me with your request," the Taoist said gravely, giving Lin Han another bow.

Relief made Lin Han sag where she stood. She'd done the right thing gathering up the ashes.

"Tell me," the Taoist said over steepled fingers, looking down at her from his tall height. "How old was your sister?"

"She was eight. Her name was Dao Ming."

The Taoist came around his counter and stood in front

of Lin Han. He bowed very low to her, then knelt down so he was closer in height to her. "I'm so sorry," he said. "But Dao Ming was born in the year of the Ox."

"She was," Lin Han said.

The lump was back in her throat.

"I cannot find a mate for her," the priest said simply.

Surprise took away some of the sting.

A grown up, speaking so plainly?

"Why not?" Lin Han said.

"She's too young. She can't even have a funeral. Veneration is only right from the young to the old. The other way, from someone older to someone so young—it isn't the natural order of things. And brides, as you know, are very honored."

"Please," Lin Han whispered. The room had suddenly grown very dark, and the medicine smells clogged the back of her throat.

"I'm sorry. But I can't help."

The Taoist reached across and turned her gently toward the door.

Lin Han felt as light as a leaf blown by the wind, no weight to push back.

Before she could think she found herself outside in the bright sunshine.

A group of boisterous students were walking by in the street, causing Lin Han to shrink back under the eaves. She stood blinking, her breath heaving.

Of course the adults couldn't help. They hadn't been able to help after the accident, when Dao Ming had been hurt.

A wailing sound startled Lin Han. She pressed her back against the rough wood of the Taoist's shop. Where was it coming from? The sound of clashing cymbals and drums rolled out next, meant to scare away any bad spirits.

From down the street she saw a group of men carrying something on sticks over their shoulders, a palanquin she assumed. Someone very important. As they drew closer, she saw she'd been wrong.

They carried a paper-wrapped wooden coffin.

On top of the coffin was a painting of the dead: a young man with stiff black hair, a sharp nose, and kind eyes.

Lin Han carefully watched the funeral procession, picking out his mother and father, his younger brothers, and the other relatives.

No wife.

As if sleep walking, Lin Han found herself drawn out of the shadows, following the procession.

She would find a mate for Dao Ming, one way or another.

White grave stone embraced the hill outside of Yen Tu. Lin Han followed at the tail of funeral, still clutching her vase. Her head felt light, like a feather fluttering across the road, while sand chained her body to the earth, heavy and slow with exhaustion.

Wailing mourners shrieked at the front of the procession, followed by the musicians banging cymbals and drums to chase away any evil spirits attracted to the dead body.

The graves nearest the entrance hadn't been cleaned in several months—probably since the last *qingming* festival that spring: leaves littered the curving white stone and bright grass marred the smooth lines.

Lin Han vowed to come out and clean her sister's memorial place every month, not to wait for the annual tomb sweeping celebration.

As Lin Han followed the procession up the hill her heart lightened. Only those with a proper rank were buried up on top of the hill. This meant the family not only had money, but power and placement.

It wouldn't matter if the family found another bride for their dead son: Lin Han would make sure he married Dao Ming first. Any other brides would be second or third wives. Not first.

The clanging cymbals and drums started to get louder, the pace, faster. Lin Han hurried, catching up to the stragglers in the procession, then pushing her way forward. No one stopped her. She didn't wear the proper white mourning clothes over her robe, but her face was still streaked with ashes and tears, so she must belong.

A Buddhist priest in bright orange robes stood at the head of the grave. He was a tall, pompous man, the kind who smiled at children but then treated them as if they couldn't understand even the simplest words.

Lin Han knew she wouldn't get any help from him.

The parents of the boy stood beside the priest. The mother wept loudly while her husband and sons consoled her. Lin Han looked at them closely.

Would they be kind to her sister?

They were kind with each other. Maybe they would welcome Dao Ming, too, if their son visited one of them in a dream and told them about his wife.

The paper-wrapped coffin sat poised over the grave,

balanced on the long poles used to carry it from the town. Alongside each pole was strung a strong rope.

When the priest finished his prayers and blessings, the laborers came forward. They slid the poles away while holding onto the ropes.

Lin Han stood poised, right beside the grave, the ashes of her sister's spirit tablet still clenched tightly to her chest.

As was custom, everyone in the funeral procession turned their back as the coffin started to disappear into the earth.

Lin Han didn't care if the laborers saw her: they wouldn't say anything, not to the family. It wasn't their place.

So she tipped the vase and scattered the ashes on top of the coffin.

Dao Ming and her intended would be buried together. Their funerals would be held together, because now all the prayers said for him would be for her as well.

It was as good an introduction between the families as any.

Lin Han waited for the priest to finish the funeral under the fragrant pine trees in the graveyard. The family was still wailing, and they were burning incense. She'd learned her sister's future-husband's name—Tu Shr. The empty vase sat beside her. She was so tired. She just wanted to sleep. But Dao Ming must be married, first.

The early afternoon breezes tugged at Lin Han's hair. She gathered twigs to her, stripped the bark down and used it to tie the sticks together, making little figures. The one with the sprig of long soft needles from a yew tree was

Dao Ming. It didn't really look like a skirt but it was the best Lin Han could do. Tu Shr's had a knotty twig across the top, like big strong shoulders.

Lin Han hid behind the tree as the procession started back down the hill. She didn't want anyone to ask her any questions. There she found the cap of an acorn that she also gathered up.

As soon as the last person had reached the bottom of the hill, Lin Han raced back up. The laborers wouldn't fill in the grave until later, closer to twilight, when light ran away from the world. In three days' time, the younger son would return and take a cup of the dirt back to the family that they would use to represent their dead son on their ancestors' altar, replacing the spirit tablet which was buried with the body.

At the edge of the grave, Lin Han found three trampled pieces of paper ghost money that hadn't been thrown into the grave, money the dead could spend in the afterlife. She wished she had more, but she couldn't climb into the grave and ever hope to get back out.

The three pieces would have to do for the bride price, what the groom's family gave the bride's.

Lin Hand made a small pile of dirt on the left side of the grave and placed the figure of Dao Ming there. She formally presented the bride price to her, wishing she had a red envelope for the money. She tucked the money in under the little figure. On the right side, she created a second pile, and placed the figure of Tu Shr there.

When everything was set, Lin Han picked up Tu Shr. Carrying him well above her head to honor him, she did a couple of dancing steps as she walked around the top of the grave to the other side.

"Look Dao Ming! The wedding procession has arrived!"

Lin Han kept Dao Ming in one hand while she hid Tu Shr in the other. It wasn't proper for the couple to see each other yet. Then she danced back to the other side.

"Dao Ming! You've arrived at your husband's house now. It's so big!"

From the top of the hill, it almost seemed that way. Tu Shr didn't control all of the graveyard and ghosts from his high point, but she could pretend.

Finally, Lin Han brought the two stick figures together on the mound of dirt. She didn't know the words the priests would say, so she sang a hymn to Xi Wang Hu, asking her for blessings on the couple: May they never grow hungry, may they have many children, and may they always be honored.

Lin Han placed the acorn cap next to Dao Ming, telling her, "Drink up! Drink your wedding cup!"

Then she placed it next to Tu Shr, telling him, "This is your bridal cup. Drink and be together forever."

Lin Han stepped back, bowed her head and closed her eyes to give the happy couple a moment of privacy.

Exhaustion slammed down on her and she swayed. The wind played with her hair, stronger now. Maybe a storm was blowing up.

When she opened her eyes, Tu Shr had slid down on the dirt mound so his head was now close to Dao Ming's.

Lin Han clapped her hands. Tu Shr had surely accepted Dao Ming as a bride! Her sister had a husband, someone who would look after her and treat her with respect.

Lin Han bowed low to the happy couple.

Normally, what followed would be the wedding feast. But there wasn't anyone else to celebrate.

"I will eat for both of you later," Lin Han promised as she picked up the figures, holding them together in the palms of her hands.

"The goddess will look out for you and bless you always," she promised as she opened her hands over the edge of the grave and let the figures tumble onto the paper coffin below.

They landed on a bit of clean paper, not where every member of the family had dropped a handful of dirt.

Lin Han gave them the acorn cup, and the ghost money as well.

She didn't know what to do with the vase. It didn't belong in the grave. She couldn't take it home: it was just one more thing of her sister's that her family would deny.

Instead, she planted it firmly at the head of the grave. Maybe when the younger son came back to get the dirt for the ancestors' altar, he'd see the vase and use it instead. That way, both Dao Ming and Tu Shr would be venerated.

After one last low bow, Lin Han turned away from the grave and started down the hill. She was too tired to skip or dance, though she knew she should—she was still part of a wedding procession.

But her feet dragged on the earth and her tears started again. No one else would ever know what she'd done, how she'd taken care of her sister.

Still. She'd finally managed to find her peace.

AUTHOR'S NOTES

I wrote this story for a workshop, while I was at a workshop. It was, and still remains, a very emotional story for me.

The instructor asked us to write about things that our family didn't talk about. The death of my sister is one of those things.

Months later, that instructor asked to include this story in the first issue of Fiction River. As it hadn't sold anywhere, I was happy for her to have it.

This story has been one of my most popular stories, and has been reprinted a few times.

THE BLOOD HOUND

The blood hound following Myrizhah flopped down in the street outside the tinker's shop Myrizhah entered. She knew better than to think the hound would grow bored and leave while she shopped. Even if she tried going out the back, or ran away on the fastest horse, it would still find her. No woman escaped the blood hounds.

Still, Myrizhah couldn't help but stop and glance through the tinker's shop window back at the hound, who lay there in the dusty dirt road like a regular dog. He was medium sized, coming up to about her knee, with short, red-brown hair and tall, pointy ears that stuck on the top of his head. His nose was black and took up a disproportional amount of his snout. His eyes were just a shade lighter than his fur. The hound looked sad and too aware, as if he had seen too many babies die.

No one bothered the hound. Most avoided him, either crossing the street or walking a wide path around him.

Despite his ordinary looks, people could *feel* that he was something special.

Myrizhah turned away, looking back into the shop. It was only lit by the window overlooking the street, making it seem dark and crowded. Hanging from the walls were small brass pans for cooking eggs, large iron kettles for stew, tiny pewter cups given to newborns, and even finely decorated tin squares that could be hung on a wall, merely for decoration.

It was a rich person's shop, despite how tiny and dimly lit it was. It smelled of clean coins, fancy brass polish, and iron shavings.

Myrizhah wasn't rich. But she wanted to give her unborn son the best.

"I see a hound's got your scent," said the tinker, coming out from behind his counter to stand beside

Myrizhah. He was an older man with many fine wrinkles around his blue eyes. He wore his white hair to his shoulders while his face was clean shaven, as was the custom here. He had a bulbous nose and flabby lips, with heavy jowls.

It was the type of face Myrizhah had gotten used to here, up north, as opposed to the knife-thin and sharp features of the men she'd grown up with in the south, with their darker skins and full beards.

"Congratulations," the tinker continued.

Myrizhah nodded and reflexively put her hand on her extended belly, as if to protect it. Blood hounds only followed pregnant women whose babies had magic.

It was considered an honor up here, in the north, to birth a baby of power. Something else that was very different from where Myrizhah had grown up.

"Ducca the midwife has declared the baby will be a boy," Myrizhah told the tinker.

"I see," the tinker said, nodding. "You want something to bind him here."

"Yes," Myrizhah said. "A horseshoe made from an ore dug in the nearby mountains."

It was custom both in the north as well as the south to place a horseshoe, the symbol of the Goddess Onnet, on the belly of a woman as she was giving birth, to help draw the baby out. In ancient times, the first letter of Onnet's name had always been carved as the symbol Ω.

A magician's magic was tied to the land, usually close to where he was born. While a magician might have some small power over all the trees, he could do amazing things within his small, local forest. A magician might have an affinity for rock, but he could only perform great magic with the granite mined in a specific range. Same with water workers, who worked best with their personal creek or lake.

This babe had to be tied here so Myrizhah could leave him behind with a clear conscience when she escaped the family she'd been married into and ran away back to the south.

The tinker cast a sly glace at Myrizhah's clothes, obviously calculating her wealth. Then his eyes rested on her belly for a moment and grew softer.

"I'd recommend a horseshoe made from the tin found near the Agrafa pass," he said kindly. Then he grew shrewd again. "Unless you'd prefer something from the silver mine…"

"Tin would do quite nicely," Myrizhah assured him.

Her mother-in-law didn't deserve a grandson who worked with silver or gold, though magicians who worked with metal were rare.

Not that her mother-in-law would have thought such fortune possible. Not from her bad luck daughter-in-law, the one who had already caused the family such grief.

The son she carried kicked suddenly, as if to distract her dark thoughts. Myrizhah couldn't help her gasp. That boy took her breath away, sometimes.

Too bad she would never see him grow up.

"May I offer you a chair, madam?" the tinker said, taking her arm.

Myrizhah stopped herself from pulling away and shouting at the man. No one in the south would ever presume to casually touch her that way.

Instead, she let herself be guided to a guest's chair that was just before the counter. Though the pillow covered in fine, red linen, it was stuffed with straw, hard and practical.

She refused the tea the tinker offered her, though she did take a cup of cool water.

The boy kicked again. The pain he offered her was almost rhythmic, though she didn't think these were contractions. Not yet. As this was her first child, she had to rely on Ducca the midwife, who told her the babe wasn't due for weeks.

Still, she put down the cool cup and started bargaining with the tinker. Though she might be short of breath, she wasn't addled, and she could still strike a good deal.

When Myrizhah left the shop, her tin horseshoe in hand, she paused for just a moment. It was bright out here, the air in the mountains cooler and drier than what she'd grown up with. The dust in the air smelled the same though, and despite their strange clothes and manners, underneath, the people here were the same too: poor and just trying to get by.

The hound had already risen, giving her that too-knowing look.

It didn't care what her plans were after the baby was born. All it cared about was the babe.

There were stories of hounds who'd "helped" during difficult births, killing the mother but saving the child.

He wouldn't get her, though. This baby would be born with ease.

Then Myrizhah was going to run away. Leave the harshness of the mountains, the softness of the trees, the rich black dirt.

Go live in the desert again.

Even if she died trying.

Ducca the midwife waited for Myrizhah at the tiny farmstead. It wasn't much bigger than a shack—just a single room with a shelf for her bed and a hearth at the back—but at least it gave Myrizhah a place to live away from the family compound where the rest of her in-laws resided.

Myrizhah knew better than to look around, to hope that her husband had returned from the war. He'd gone off just after they'd discovered she'd become pregnant, with a cheery promise that he'd return in a month, having made his fortune as promised by the *Padisha-i-Ghazi*, the great emperor.

News of his death had made her mother in law, as well as the rest of the family, turn cold to his foreign wife.

Myrizhah understood. They thought she was bad luck.

The fact that she was carrying a son, as well as a magician, had warmed their reception of her only slightly. They were still regularly awful to her, and she wept many hidden tears.

Ducca took one look at Myrizhah then took her by the arm, bringing her closer to the fire.

Myrizhah couldn't help but stiffen. Did everyone have to touch her today?

Ducca was a tiny woman, barely coming up to Myrizhah's ample breasts. Myrizhah always felt like one of the giantesses from the tales standing next to her. However, Myrizhah could also feel the strength in Ducca's hands, how firmly she held Myrizhah. This was no weak, pampered woman.

Ducca wore her blonde hair braided. It shone like gold in the firelight. Just like her husband's had. It had been one of the reasons why Myrizhah had agreed to marry him, to travel so far north, away from her family and everything she knew.

She still hoped his son would have that fine, golden hair.

"This babe is as impatient as you are," Ducca chided. "He's dropped." She reached for Myrizhah's belly, then paused before she touched her. "May I?" she asked.

Myrizhah nodded. Though it wasn't proper for a stranger to touch a woman, this was a midwife. And she did need to know the condition of her charge.

Ducca's strong fingers probed Myrizhah's belly.

Myrizhah kept her mouth closed firmly as she felt the nausea rise.

"The head's down," Ducca told her. "He's coming. Tomorrow or the next day."

Myrizhah nodded, relieved and anxious at the same time. She hadn't finished her preparation. She did have a bundle of travel clothes already prepared. When she'd leave would depend on how quickly she'd recover her strength. If she didn't have to hold the babe, she knew it would be easier to leave him, but she'd never seen a woman just walk away from a birth.

"Have you named him yet?" Ducca asked.

Myrizhah shrugged. She'd told her in-laws early on that it was her people's custom not to speak the name of an unborn out loud, not until after they were born. It was too easy for a curse to be put on the unborn.

It was an old wives' tale. However, Myrizhah didn't believe in curses, not like that. She'd never given the baby a name because she'd never wanted to be that close to the boy.

She was only going to bear him. Then she was going to leave.

Ducca crossed her arms over her chest and scowled. She wore short sleeves that showed off her muscular arms, along with what they called "trous," full pants that looked like a long skirt. She shook her head. "You'll change your mind when the babe is born," she said softly.

Myrizhah raised herself up to her full height. "What are you talking about?" she asked disdainfully.

"You'll come to love the boy," Ducca told her.

Mryizhah merely blinked at the midwife, unsure how to reply. She wasn't going to be there long enough to love him. Then she shrugged. "I'm told that happens," she said.

Ducca nodded. "I have promised to go to Farmer Tiegan's house, to check on his wife. I only promised because I had thought your son was weeks away, not days." She scowled at Myrizhah's belly, as if the boy was purposefully vexing her.

"Go," Myrizhah told her. "I'll be fine."

"I could stop at the main house, get your mother-in-law or one of your sister-in-laws to sit with you," Ducca offered.

"No," Myrizhah said immediately. "Not until the birth is closer," she added when she saw Ducca's shocked look at her strong refusal.

"All right," Ducca said. "I won't be long. I promise."

Myrizhah knew the woman prided herself on her keeping her word. She was always directly honest with everyone. Myrizhah found it off putting at times, refreshing at others.

Ducca had no children of her own. Which may have been why she was so concerned with others having healthy births.

"I have the hound here to help as well," Myrizhah said with dark humor.

Ducca glanced over toward the door of the tiny farmstead. The hound was waiting on the threshold as always, in his usual guard spot.

Before the baby was born, he would protect Myrizhah. That was true of all the blood hounds.

After the baby had started coming was an entirely different matter.

"I'll be back so you won't need his help," Ducca said earnestly. She threw a cloak over her shoulders and hurried out the door.

The room seemed colder without her presence. Myrizhah carefully picked up another piece of wood and threw it on fire. Pregnant women were supposed to be warm all the time, but Myrizhah was cold up here in the north, where the sun was so pale.

Soon, she would be warm again, back in her own southern home. Her family wouldn't necessarily welcome her back with grand feasts of pomegranates and fruit wine —she should stay with her husband's family, even if she found them intolerable. But she hoped she'd be less unwelcome there.

Myrizhah thought she'd spin a little more by the firelight but found her eyes drooping. Instead, she laid down on the tiny shelf and napped, instantly dreaming of holding the tiny tin horseshoe like a dowsing rod in her hands as she marched across endless sands, but the tin had no affinity for the land and it couldn't lead her to water, no matter how far she roamed.

Pain.

Myrizhah dreamed of an iron poker shoved into her belly, the pain of it making her cry out.

When she opened her bleary eyes, the pain didn't recede. It took her a moment to place the dark wooden roof above her head, not the canvas of tents or the stucco of the towns.

She was in the north, where it was always cold, with a family who hated her and would just as soon she died in childbirth.

Not that her mother-in-law had said such a thing directly to Myrizhah. However, the woman had refused to pray for her and only said prayers for the unborn son.

He was the only thing of value to them, and only if he turned out to be powerful.

They would all soon find out.

The child was on its way.

Myrizhah had no idea what time it was. Had she been asleep for hours? Or a fraction of that time?

Another rolling wave of pain washed over her. Powerful contractions emanated from her nether regions and up her belly.

Yes, this boy was as impatient as his father had been the first time they'd lain together as man and wife, taking her roughly, then drying her tears and doing it the right way, as a real man should, with tenderness.

There was nothing tender about birth, though.

Ducca had taught Myrizhah a rhyming song to help her to breathe through the contractions.

Myrizhah hadn't bothered to tell the midwife that unlike her northern sisters, she knew how to count far past the fingers on her hand. Still, she tried to hum the song as she slowed down her breathing, getting ready for the first awful push.

Something cold touched Myrizhah's hand, bringing her back from the world of pain. Turning her head took a monumental effort, but she still managed to peer out beyond the edge of the bed.

The hound stood there, dark and glowering.

"Oh no," Myrizhah said. "You don't get to help. I can manage this on my own."

Then another contraction hit and the room grew dark.

Myrizhah knew there was something wrong. She'd seen childbirth before, had held her eldest sister's hand to help ease her through it.

There was too much pain. The blankets beneath her were soaked with too much blood.

Myrizhah hadn't done any stitching for the last four weeks. Nothing should be blocking the birth canal.

But that was how it felt. As if the baby couldn't get out.

Myrizhah cried out as the next wave hit her. She had to do something, anything. Or she might take a knife to her own belly to end this.

Wait. Where was the horseshoe? She'd gone to sleep holding it.

The metal felt cool to Myrizhah's sweating palm. She raised up her tunic and slid the horseshoe onto her belly.

The pain doubled, the horseshoe sticking to her skin as she writhed.

What had the tinker given her? Had he poisoned the metal? She couldn't pull it off—it stuck to her skin as if glued there.

Myrizhah wailed in grief. She had to live. Had to see the desert again. Had to get this baby born.

Coolness touched her fingers again.

With horror, Myrizhah looked to the side.

The hound was there, looming. He had grown bigger than the medium-sized dog he had always appeared to be, and now would come up to her waist, easily. His coat had changed as well, growing black as a curse.

"No!" Myrizhah screamed as the hound grew taller. He placed one paw—now larger than her own hand—on the side of the bed shelf. He lowered his muzzle to her belly, his hot breath easing her pain for the moment.

Myrizhah braced herself for the next part—when the hound tore her belly to bits, killing her in order to save the boy.

Instead, the hound licked her belly, licked at the tin horseshoe, drawing it up in his mouth, much more delicately than Myrizhah would have expected.

Suddenly, Myrizhah could breathe again. The pain instantly lessened.

What had the tinker given her?

A whining noise made Myrizhah look to her right, to where the hound stood.

He had turned the horseshoe, holding the curve so the tin ends stuck out from his mouth like odd-shaped fangs. Then, the hound shook his head. He moved so quickly his head became a blur.

A soft *pop* filled the room when the hound stopped, as though a cork on a barrel of beer had just been loosened.

The horseshoe was no longer tin.

The hound raised himself back up, carefully placing one paw on the bed shelf, then putting the horseshoe back on Myrizhah's belly. It felt cool against her skin and the pain receded another fraction.

Myrizhah craned her neck to see the horseshoe, running her fingers along its smooth surface.

It was now made of clear glass shot through with ribbons of gold and green.

The colors of the old kings. Before the *Padisha-i-Ghazi*, the magician emperor, had come to power centuries before.

Then another wave of pain struck Myrizhah. It was a normal pain, though. Something she'd seen other women bear as part of childbirth.

With a determined cry, Myrizhah pushed, as impatient as the babe to have the birth finished.

The head crowned with her next push. It was too late for Myrizhah to stagger over to the birthing chair so she could at least catch the baby with her arms. Instead, she gave another great push, the shoulders sliding out followed by the rest of him.

It took all the stubbornness Myrizhah had to make herself sit up, to reach for her babe, to awkwardly draw it up across her sore stomach.

The hound licked at the boy's foot, causing him to jerk and cry, drawing in his first breath, letting loose with a healthy wail.

"Shhh, shh," Myrizhah said, cradling the boy's head.

She didn't care for the boy. She couldn't. But she could hold him and comfort him, just this once.

A shadow crossed her sight.

The hound had levered himself up to the side of the bed again, looking down on her.

He seemed to be asking her permission.

Myrizhah collected the boy's feet up higher on her body and gave the hound a sharp nod.

One giant paw reached out and pressed on her belly, hard.

Myrizhah couldn't help but shout with pain once again

as her body had yet another contraction. The afterbirth came sputtering out.

The hound moved from the side of the bed to the foot, where he greedily devoured the afterbirth. Then he looked up at her, licking his bloodied chops.

Padisha-i-Ghazi thanks you for your contribution.

Then the hound disappeared, a great wind chasing him.

Myrizhah shivered. She was going to have to clean up this mess, soon. Clip the umbilical cord. Say the prayers to Onnet, thanking her for the live birth, the healthy son.

Then she realized what the hound had said.

He would go directly to the emperor and vomit up the afterbirth. Then the emperor would take a piece of the afterbirth and fashion it into a scale, that would be sewn into the great cloak he always wore.

No magician could attack the emperor in his cloak. They couldn't harm their own blood.

This was why the blood hounds had been conjured. To protect the emperor.

For the hound to speak to her meant that her boy was a magician of great power. That the emperor himself would one day fear.

Then Myrizhah looked down at the boy.

He had both hands clenched tightly around the glass horseshoe, resting his cheek against it.

With a sinking feeling, Myrizhah realized that she was going to have to take the boy with her when she left.

Metal, stone, iron—these were the materials the northern magicians had an affinity for.

Glass—basically sand blasted with such heat that it melted—was a material that only a southern magician could use.

He could only come to power in her lands.

She would have to name him now.

Maybe Alpheais, after his father. Or Trulliç, after hers.

She could decide later.

For now, she could sleep, rest a little, content that she would be going home.

AUTHOR'S NOTES

I deliberately wrote *The Blood Hound* to explore and create the world of the Tanesh Empire. The original had a few different things with the magic system as well as the hierarchy of magicians.

However, most of what I wrote became the world of the first book, *The Glass Magician.*

I included this story because again, it's a way of seeing how a short story can be such a large spring board for a much longer piece.

THE FAIRY BOY BAND

Oswald sat, ensconced in his favorite chair, next to the cheerily burning fireplace. He had a glass of his favorite scotch warming on the small end table beside him. The snifter was also a favorite: antique, hand-blown Tiffany glassware, with an indentation on one side that fit his thumb perfectly when he picked up the glass and swirled the amber liquor. His dad had given Oswald a full set of them for his thirtieth birthday, then died of a heart attack unexpectedly just a year later, which made Oswald cherish the glasses even more.

The scent of Oswald's simple dinner of poached salmon in white wine and dill lingered in the air, though overlaid now with the smell of woodsy, pine smoke. Oswald still wore his office clothes—plain blue long-sleeved shirt and tan-colored slacks—but he'd taken his shoes off and donned his heaviest wool socks to ward off the chill of the autumn evening.

Everything was perfect. Silence surrounded him, so welcome after the hectic day in the office where he worked as a quality engineer, testing the code of morons. He had a new book to read—a fascinating non-fiction work about the history of pixie engineering. He was settled in for the night, no lights on in his living room except for the fire (loving his electronic book reader!), and at peace. No girlfriend badgering him, no new video games demanding to be played, no awkward social situation that he needed to engage in for his work.

Nope. Just him, a book, a good scotch, and the quiet of the evening.

Until the damned music started to play.

Oswald tried to ignore the tinkling, which to his ears sounded like the musician tapped on a series of icicles, going from tiny to large, testing their tone but all of them annoyingly tinny. Then came the sweeping flute, the trilling noises worse than claws down a chalkboard, making him shiver.

Of course, tonight the band had added some sort of bass that sounded like frogs belching and farting.

With a huge, put upon sigh, Oswald set his reader on the end table and picked up his scotch again. He couldn't go complain to the fairies making music in his backyard that he had a headache again. They didn't have to accommodate him every time he made that excuse, and he'd much rather save it for when he *was* actually ill.

The arrangement with the fairies had all been written out in clear language in the agreement that he'd signed when he'd bought his house. He owned the building and the land it sat on, though he had to check with the neighborhood home owner's association (HOA) first before he painted his house or added large decorations. He could use his house and the land as he saw fit during the day and early evening. If he gave adequate notice, he could also use the yard later at night, say, for a celebration or ritual.

However, the fairies owned the backyard starting one hour after true night had fallen, which meant during the fall and winter, like now, they'd start playing their damned music earlier and earlier.

He'd complained to the association about the racket the fairies made every night. The association came by and merely ensured that the fairies were in compliance with "quiet hours." Now, the stupid band started their jam session strictly on time, one hour after full dark, as well as ended exactly at 11:00 P.M.

Oswald had no ideas that fairies could be so punctual —they tended to work on their own, "fairy" time. He did know they could be assholes. He'd worked with one for a while, a stupid prima donna developer who'd believed his code was perfect and never needed to be tested.

Thankfully, the idiot had left to form his own company. (Oswald would never admit to how small his soul was and how gleefully he'd watched the asshole's company sink.)

Fairies had always lived beside humanity, along with brownies and pixies. (Elves, trolls, vampires, and all the other creatures man had documented over the years had turned out to be just myths, thankfully, even though the consensus about ghosts was far from unanimous.) However, it hadn't been until the civil rights movement in the 1960s that the FBP (fairies, brownies, pixies) came forward and demanded equal rights as well.

The denial had been truly epic, particularly on the part of the US Government. The backlash had been immediate as well. However, after the All Races riots in the 1970s, an accord was signed and everyone went back to making gobs of money in the 1980s—including the fairies and other races.

However, while the FBP could all cast glamours and appear to be human-sized, in reality, they didn't grow much taller than up to a man's knee. They had no use for houses, cars, or TV, living on the magical plane. They did like the internet, and Oswald had once seen a commercial for a documentary about FBP online addiction.

So the FBP frequently worked out deals like the one Oswald had signed, time-sharing yards, parks, or wilderness areas. They also paid rent, keeping the area tidy and beautiful, which made the properties cheaper. It also meant that no one littered anymore: fairies would likely take any trash a human dumped in one of their areas and make it magically appear inside the human's house at the most inopportune moment.

While there had been talk of forming an environmental protection agency, once the FBP came forward, there was no need. They wouldn't allow land to be despoiled anymore. Any grand engineering scheme the humans came up with, like oil pipelines or drilling offshore, had to be okayed by the FBP. Of course, greedy corporations tried to get around that, only to have their operations plagued with inexplicable accidents, so many that they'd end up scrapping the project.

The air Oswald breathed was crystal clean and fresh. The sidewalks he walked down were empty of trash. He'd heard that in areas where the FBP weren't as well liked or as well integrated, people without homes actually lived on the streets. He couldn't imagine that. The FBP had been good for humanity, in general.

However, he hated the racket the fairies who lived in his backyard made. Every. Single. Night. It was driving him batty. They played the same songs over and over again, practicing.

What could he do to evict them?

The next morning, while waiting for his garlic bagels to finish toasting, Oswald checked online for FBP neighborhood "support" groups. What he found turned his stomach. He wasn't a racist, or a species-ist, not like those crazy people. And he wasn't about to move to Alabama or some such "humans only" state, though how in the hell people were able to ensure that, he had no idea.

There was an old joke about fairies breeding like

bunnies. The truth was that there was no place in the world immune from their influence.

Oswald's own HOA had been useless regarding getting the noise turned down. He spread cream cheese on his bagel, then set it aside and let it melt while he poured himself a cup of coffee from the automated pot on his kitchen counter.

He knew he couldn't get rid of the fairies, as much as he might like to. He'd thought about buying huge, six foot tall speakers and using them to blast music into the backyard and drown out the fairy music.

However, that didn't actually get rid of his problem. He wanted less noise, not more. He'd looked into noise cancelation headphones, but none of those would guarantee blocking the music of the fey, which operated on more than just human dimensions.

Oswald continued doing random searches on the internet while he stood at the kitchen counter eating his breakfast. He looked at fairy bands (who knew that fairy boy-bands were so popular?), equipment for dealing with fairy noise (all of it designed to part a fool from his money) as well as old myths for dealing with fairies, like leaving out a thimbleful of milk and cookie crumbs (though fairies appeared to prefer cake crumbs to cookies).

As Oswald rinsed off his dishes, he thought about the last time he'd gone out to try to get the fairies to shut up. Fairies lived to be about a hundred years old, and unless they were using a glamour, tended to look their age. In addition, the younger fairies glowed with a particularly clean white light. From all the inter-species classes Oswald had been required to attend from grade school onward, he knew that older fairies had a more yellowish glow to them.

The lead singer Oswald had talked with had been

young, with a searing white glow. Oswald would have put him in his early twenties. He had a very pale face with a sharp nose and chin. He'd dyed his hair green and worn a torn T-shirt in a futile attempt to look tough. His wings had been amazing, though, iridescent blue and gold, more like a dragonfly's wings than an angel's. (Fairies always appeared with their wings no matter what size or shape they took. No one really understood if it was racial pride or trait even glamours couldn't disguise.)

The lead singer had also been incredibly argumentative, not wanting to hear any of Oswald's complaints, claiming that they'd been their first and that they'd only permitted Oswald to live there.

The fairy had been very careful not to make any threats. Fairies were good with language that way.

Maybe Oswald could talk to the head of the fairies in the neighborhood. He wasn't getting anywhere with the kids. His HOA had a fairy liaison he could schedule a meeting with. Oswald had merely talked with the human representative before.

Perhaps, if Oswald could speak with another adult, he could finally get some peace and quiet.

He scheduled an appointment online, for later that evening, at Margaret's Coffee Shop, just down the street.

It made him feel better as he waited for the company bus to take him to his job. He was finally taking positive steps instead of hiding in his house, shaking with rage.

Then again, if this didn't work, maybe he would try one of those illegal sonic disrupters that would force the fairies to leave.

Oswald hurried from the bus stop directly to the coffee shop. He'd planned on arriving early, but traffic had thwarted him. Luckily, he was close to being on time, within a few minutes.

The shop door banged open as Oswald rushed in. The barista standing behind the counter that ran along the right wall glared at him, though no one else appeared to notice. To his left, over a dozen tables spread out across the bare concrete floor, most of them occupied with either FBP or humans, chatting and laughing. Two balls of rainbow-colored light, each about the size of a volleyball, flitted above a pair of older fairies sitting at the back—very young, small fairies, playing. Beside them stood a tiny, empty stage, with posters advertising local bands playing on the weekends as well as an upcoming poetry slam.

A glowering, older fairy sat by himself at a table very close to the entrance. Oswald rushed over and asked expectantly, "Are you Francesco?"

The fairy looked up. He had a pushed in face, like a pug, with black eyes and hair. He looked Hispanic, with dark skin and broad features. Even his hands appeared meaty where they lay on the table. His wings, too, appeared yellowed and aged. He wore a dark blue T-shirt that showed more chest muscles than the usual fairy, and clean blue jeans, with black work boots.

Was this how he really looked? Or was it some elaborate glamour to make him seem like a working class dude?

"Frank," the fairy said in a voice that was much deeper than Oswald expected.

"Can I get you anything?" Oswald asked, gesturing toward the empty counter where the barista still glared at him, expectant.

"Two crumb cakes," Frank said after a moment.

"Sure thing. Coming right up," Oswald said, trying to hide his excitement. Was this a way to bribe the fairy? Maybe get him to see reason?

Oswald ordered himself a hot mocha and two cakes for Frank, then stayed at the counter, watching the barista carefully. She seemed like the type to spit in a drink if she decided she didn't like you. And right now, Oswald would swear that she not only hated all of humanity but every single creature on the planet. The hair curling around her face radiated rage. Her dark skin looked flushed, and her broad features appeared chiseled in angry stone.

But she made his drink competently enough, even added extra whipped cream without charging him for it. It was far beyond her to smile or act polite. However, she did wear a nametag that labeled her as "Margret" and the coffee shop was named "Margret's Coffee Shop." Was she the owner?

Oswald hurried back with his goodies to the table where Frank sat. Margaret had served the cakes on a small pewter plate that easily fit into Oswald's palm. The cakes, too, were tiny, about as big as the end of Oswald's thumb. They were made with almond meal, lavender, and honey.

After Oswald took off his coat, he realized that Frank was waiting for him to say something.

"Thank you for meeting me, tonight," Oswald said hurriedly.

"I don't have a lot of time," Frank replied. He broke the tiny golden cake in front of him into pieces, scattering the crumbs. Then he pressed his thumb onto the plate, picking up the crumbs and licking them off.

Oswald tried not to be grossed out by the fairy's eating habits. He reminded himself that no matter how large this

Frank may appear, he was actually tiny, and more than mere crumbs wouldn't fit into his mouth.

"Then I'll get right to the point," Oswald said. "I have this fairy band who plays music in my backyard every night."

Frank pierced him with a sharp look. "They playing outside of regular haunting hours?" he asked.

"No, but they make such a racket! Every single night," Oswald said. "Surely we could work out a deal where they only played a few nights a week." He would prefer for them to go play somewhere else, *anywhere* else, but he knew he couldn't just insist that they vacate.

"What would you offer?" Frank asked. He didn't sound sympathetic, but at least he'd asked, instead of saying it was impossible, like the HOA rep had.

"I don't know," Oswald said. He hadn't considered what the fairies might want from him. "I could supply crumb cakes or something." How much was his peace and quiet worth? How much would the fairies try to bleed him dry?

"Case of dew-drop wine, delivered every fortnight," Frank said after a moment.

Oswald gulped. He couldn't afford that! A single bottle cost about what he made in a day, and he made a very good wage working in IT.

"A bottle, once a month," Oswald countered. He'd never been good at bargaining, though he knew he must.

Frank snorted. "Don't waste my time. A full case. Every fourteen days."

"What exactly would I get if I could meet your price?" Oswald asked. He knew he'd have to spell everything out exactly. Fairies were notoriously tricky that way.

A look of cunning crossed Frank's face. "Music every other night," he said.

"No," Oswald said. "That's still too much. Music once a week, for two bottles a month."

Frank shook his head. "Not worth it," he said.

"What do you mean?" Oswald asked as Frank licked more crumbs away. God, he wasn't about to lick the plate clean, was he?

Frank pierced him with a look. "You know that if they aren't practicing in your yard, they'll set up a garage in the fairy lands and play?" He shuddered. "The agreement lets them play here, so they aren't driving their parents batty with the noise. If you want them to play elsewhere, you've got to make it worth our while."

Oswald gulped. Crap. He couldn't afford the bribe Frank wanted, not without going into debt. While fairies normally would negotiate, he knew Frank wouldn't budge.

"Can't you just make them stop?" Oswald asked.

Frank rolled his eyes at him. "Have you ever tried to get a teenager to do what you wanted?"

Oswald opened his mouth than closed it again. He didn't have kids, had never wanted them. On the other hand, coders frequently behaved like a bunch of juvenile delinquents. He felt Frank's pain.

"Then how am I going to get some peace and quiet?" Oswald asked.

Frank shrugged and stood up. "Your problem, human. Not ours." The fairy suddenly shrank back down as he lifted off the ground, hovering directly in front of Oswald's face. "The agreement you signed states that as long as the kids stick to the quiet hours, they get to play. Nothing you can do about it. You can't make us."

With that, Frank flitted off, passing through the glass door of the shop like a shot.

Oswald felt himself grinding his teeth. Damn it! What was he going to do?

"I hate it when they do that."

Oswald turned around to look up at Margaret. She still glared at the closed door. "Did you see the way the glass shakes? I'm always afraid that they're going to shatter it. God, I hate the FBP some days."

Oswald nodded in sympathy. "Was there something in particular they did to you today?" he asked. He normally wouldn't have engaged her, or anyone. But he felt like grousing with another human about the injustice of it all, as well as the awfulness of all fairies.

Margaret nodded. "The fairy band I had scheduled to have play here for the next couple months just broke up. They can't get their shit together long enough to send even one of the fairies to play an acoustic set or anything." She grimaced. "I had a bunch of publicity lined up and everything."

Oswald blinked, surprised. Why in the hell would she want any sort of fairy music in her café? The question must have showed on his face.

"Fairy music gets on my nerves too, but they sure draw a crowd. And they're cheap to feed. I make a good profit," Margaret said.

Oswald nodded, a plan forming, his day suddenly brightening. "I might be able to help…"

Oswald stood at the back of the packed coffee shop as the band, *Nimby*, took the stage. The "xylophone" that one member of the band played was, in fact, made out of what looked like icicles, glistening blue and white spikes that hung in the air in front of her. The lead singer strutted around on the tiny stage like a testosterone-driven frat boy, playing his flute suggestively and making at least the girl fairies swoon. Oswald had no idea what to call the instrument the bass player had. It looked like a combination bagpipe and sitar, that he strummed, squeezed, and blew on all at the same time.

Margaret gave him the thumbs up from behind the counter, though she was too busy to talk with him. She'd even had to hire extra help for the evenings the band played.

As part of their agreement, Oswald always took in the first five minutes of "music" before returning to his peace and quiet. He wasn't sure why the fairies had insisted on that in their negotiations.

But seeing how he and Margaret were getting along and chatting almost every day, perhaps it wasn't the worst condition.

He'd been more than happy to agree to find them other gigs, once this one ended, as long as they stayed out of backyard most nights. They'd even given him a cut of their take, just one percent, to make it worth his time.

Plus, the band seemed to treat him differently, now. They ran their playlists by him, letting him change the order of the songs so they didn't get monotonous, taking his suggestions of mixing fast songs with slow ones so they'd appeal to a wider audience.

The music itself still set his teeth on edge. It was worse than two cats in heat fighting, yowling, squeaking, and hissing. He'd never get used to it—hipsters who claimed they were "into" FBP bands were lying. The music of the fey was unsettling to humans: that was just their nature.

Oswald stayed for two whole songs before disappearing back into the late fall night. Leaves swirled around his feet, dancing to the tune of the winds. The crisp air filled his lungs and nipped at his nose and cheeks. He was so looking forward to a peaceful evening at home!

He hurried on his way, already tasting the smoky scotch he planned on pouring.

Except that a young fairy boy awaited him, standing on his doorstep and looking forlorn.

"Can I help you?" Oswald said as he walked up the short sidewalk to his door.

The boy looked up. He had golden, spiky hair, dark skin, and blue-green eyes that shone with sadness. "Can you help me too?" he asked. Only then did he pull down the guitar he'd had slung across his back. "I'm a singer/songwriter," he explained, strumming a chord.

Oswald couldn't help his shiver. Though it was a human instrument, the sound still carried echoes of dark dances in fairyland.

"I'm looking for a place to gig," the boy explained after another few chords. "Can you help me?"

"Pop music?" Oswald asked after the boy played a few bouncy chords.

He sniffed, insulted. "Indie. Can you help? Find me a place to play?"

Oswald blinked. His future suddenly unfurled before him.

Music manager for the fey. He'd still be working for prima donnas, but he was used to that.

"I'll meet you in the backyard," Oswald said after a moment. He knew better than to invite any fairy across the threshold of his house. "Maybe we can arrange something."

After the boy turned and started trundling around the house, Oswald hurried inside, poured himself a snifter full of scotch, then poured out a few drops of milk into a handy thimble.

Margaret surely knew other coffee shop owners who wanted exotic music. There were always hipster weddings, too. And dance parties.

The possibilities were endless.

Even if it meant he'd be dealing with fairies and having to listen to their damned music for the rest of his life.

AUTHOR'S NOTES

I wrote this story for the Uncollected Anthology issue *Mystical Melodies*.

Uncollected Anthology is a group of writers who love fantasy and each other's writing. Every three months, the authors pick a theme and write a short story for that theme.

I enjoyed this story so much that I have ended up writing a bunch of stories in what I call the NIMBY-verse. For the most part, they're all silly and funny, though some of them have turned "surprisingly deep" as it were.

DRAGON'S SON

"You want me to do what?"

Long Yen stood and drew himself up to his full height, staring down at the still seated, court-appointed white lawyer in his fancy gray suit.

The rocking hum of the air regulator sounded loud in the small space. Beyond the blond lawyer, who sat placidly with his hands folded on the scarred and rusted metal table, was the single door out of the windowless room.

It didn't matter if the door was locked, or if the lawyer and the guards had been careless. Long Yen couldn't take three steps down the hall before the emergency bells would ring, sending the miners scurrying out of the miles of corridors in the station and to their rooms. All the containment doors would slam shut, and when the authorities figured out which corridor Long Yen ran through, they'd lock him in, suck all the air out, and that would be that.

Even if Long Yen managed, somehow, to get outside, to the surface, it wouldn't be any better. Being a fugitive wasn't the problem: being topside was. It was possible to live there, just like it was possible to eat the recycling plant's sludge directly, before it had been given flavor and color and shape. He knew he was smart enough to be able to find a stronghold, join them sifting through the rough red dirt. But in that scenario, all he had was the slimmest chance that he'd find a trace of the precious minerals The Company hollowed out the planet for.

It was a life, but it wasn't really living.

"Yes, I can help you, Long Yen-san."

Long Yen narrowed his eyes at the lawyer. Given his flabbiness, he'd probably been born off planet. He'd obviously never worked the mines or corridors, not with his clean nails and unpocked face. Long Yen would bet that this lawyer had never been to the Chinese half of the station before, either. Where ever he was from, all Asians probably looked alike to him, and he hadn't bothered to learn that the planet of Da Chuan had been settled by Chinese a century ago, not Japanese.

"*Shur*," Long Yen instructed, folding his arms over his chest to hold his anger in, squeezing his calloused fingers against the scratchy prison jumpsuit. "*Yen-san* is Japanese. *Shur, Laoshur,* is Chinese."

The man's round blue eyes widened.

It would have been funny, and maybe Long Yen would have instructed him more, if he'd been at the Temple Bar, drinking with his cousins.

Here, it just made the load of rock between Long Yen and the surface feel heavier, the pumped in air a bit more stale. It reminded his aching heart that he'd never see his grandmother again, never know if the latest treatment had cured her.

"I apologize. Please forgive me, honorable *shur*." The lawyer pressed his hands together and bowed his head low —once, twice.

Long Yen sighed and didn't bother correcting the man's tone. "Whatever," he said, slumping back down into his chair again.

"Please, let me help you," the man said.

"Why should I believe you?" Long Yen said. He'd never heard of a court-appointed attorney even making an effort like this.

"Because I can get you out of here."

"By me telling you everything," Long Yen said flatly. "Everything about my family." *About the dragon's sons.*

The stranger leaned closer across the table, as if to speak a confidence.

Long Yen rolled his eyes. The hardened black ring embedded in the concrete ceiling in the corner heard every word, recorded every move. There was no privacy in an interrogation room. Even if Long Yen had a disrupter, there may have been duplicate, backup systems.

The man impatiently beckoned Long Yen closer.

With a sigh, Long Yen leaned forward as well.

"I found a loophole. Between the *qing lü* and the colony code."

Long Yen blinked, surprised. How did this stranger know about the ancient laws that the colony's code was based on?

For the first time, Long Yen felt a sliver of hope.

"You have such strong fingers, *xiao zi*," Nei Nei said, giving Long Yen a toothless grin over the tiny kitchen table.

The fan over her left shoulder made more noise than breeze in the sweltering kitchen. Dishes crowded the shelves on the walls, and the illegal ice box hummed only to itself in the corner, not connected to the station's systems.

Long Yen picked up another neon blue strand from the piles of glass-drawn wires strewn between them. The bright colors made them easy to see and weave, even in the dim light. He pushed back the hair dripping into his eyes, rubbing his fist across his sweating forehead, before he started to weave in the new strand, strengthening the net of electronic fibers.

The colors told him which way they ran. The red and blue were the weft, while the orange and black were the warp. He tried to be careful and not run his fingers along the wire: it would leave cuts all across his skin.

"*Xiao zi ma?*" Long Yen asked, pretending to concentrate, biting his lips together to keep from smiling as he teased his grandmother. "Just a boy?" Even though he had only turned seven, he felt much older and wiser than any of the boys who raced down the corridors just outside, who were Chinese, but not *family*.

"*Wo xiao zi,*" Nei Nei replied immediately. "My boy. My clever, clever boy."

Long Yen peeked up at Nei Nei suspiciously, but she still gave him a happy grin.

Maybe he was doing it right this time.

He pushed the strands together, drawing the weft along the warp, as Nei Nei had taught him. Soon, he tied off the ends and handed the net to his grandmother.

Nei Nei pulled on her work gloves and held the net up close to her face to examine the pattern. "*Hau, hau*, good," she said, nodding. "Now bring me my bag of plugs. Hurry!"

Sharp pins and needles pricked Long Yen's foot as soon as he put it on the scratched concrete floor. He'd been sitting too long on the hard metal kitchen stool. He shook his leg once, then stepped down on it hard, refusing to limp as he scurried across the room.

He knew better than to dawdle.

The bag of plugs was all the way on the other side of the room, next to the thin, fold-out futon that Nei Nei slept on. Normally, she kept the bag beside her at all times.

When the rough nylon straps pulled cruelly on Long Yen's fingers, he realized why. The wires he'd been working with had drawn unseen cuts across his flesh.

He'd forgotten a step in the process.

This was Nei Nei's way of teaching him to remember. She'd taught him early how to use the pain to help him focus.

The ache in Long Yen's foot receded while the fire in his hands grew.

Nei Nei still gave him her toothless grin, which looked innocent enough. He only now realized that her eyes were hard and merciless.

Still, Long Yen didn't drop the bag, or put it on the ground and tug it across the floor after him. He got it all the way to the table and even set it down lightly. Only then did he look at his hands and the ugly welts crisscrossing his palms, the chemicals of the bag reacting to the glass coating of the wires.

"What do I always say about wire work?" Nei Nei asked as she pawed through her bag.

"Sanitize everything," Long Yen said, turning toward the sink. Not just because of the cross-contamination, but to hide their not-always-legal work from The Company men.

He half expected Nei Nei to tell him it was too late, since he'd already been contaminated, he may as well just stay and help. But she didn't call him back. He found the grimy tube of sanitizing wash stashed under the sink, tucked in next to the antibiotic spray and black-market bandages. He carefully rationed out a small pearl of it into his reddened palm before he spread its soothing, cool gel over his burning hands.

Long Yen moved back to the table to watch Nei Nei wire the battery in. It was opaque, like the windows on the dawn side of the planet, as thin as the sheet Long Yen slept under, and as long as his thumb.

"Where do you think we'll catch the best signal?" Nei Nei asked as she worked.

"Council room kitchen hallway," Long Yen said. His heart beat harder in his chest as the silence between them spun out, only disturbed by the sound of the rocking fan in the small kitchen.

"Bold," Nei Nei finally replied.

Long Yen had tried to calculate the risks and rewards, as Nei Nei had taught him. He was pleased that she approved of his idea.

"Ceiling?" she asked as she pinched the ends of the battery and drew it longer, making it fit better along the side of the net.

"Behind the recycling pipe. The outgoing channel." People threw things they shouldn't into the recycle chutes all the time. No one would think it strange that a tiny electronic current showed up there.

"Clever monkey."

Long Yen bit his lips together and didn't reply, didn't let himself react.

The *bizi*, the white boys he'd met on one of his daring explorations of the other half of the station, had called him a monkey. But he was no *honzi*.

True, a monkey could climb the wall to get to the pipe, but only a *tian she* could worm its way behind the pipe, snake along the passage unseen.

Only a true dragon's son could tap into the communications network for the entire station with a simple woven net and not get caught.

Long Yen listened to the white lawyer (Ken? John?) recite

code and verse of the *qing lü* as well as Nei Nei or any of the other hall lawyers. He kept his eyes narrowed and his lips pressed firmly against each other, not showing the slightest bit of emotion. He'd worked hard to eliminate all his tells, precisely for a time like this.

"So you see," the lawyer (Tom?) ended with. "Section 3.14, paragraph 7, implies that the supplicant can be freed."

Long Yen spread his hands out across the tough metal table. It was too warm in the room for it to be cool, but old habits of always seeking the coldest spot died hard.

"'Freed' could be interpreted any number of ways," Long Yen said slowly, considering. "Like freed from the prison of life, if they took a Buddhist approach." That's what Nei Nei had always said, and what she'd asked for if she kept getting sicker, if the treatments didn't work.

"That's where the *Xi* code comes in," the lawyer said eagerly. "It's been applied against the *qing lü* before, for exactly such an interpretation."

"It won't work," Long Yen said, considering the possibilities. "No, the council lawyers will tell you that you've been tricked by the *bi sai*, the shell game. The family—" he paused, realizing that he'd just admitted that there was a group, something beyond just him. "*My* family, has too many pieces in play. The council lawyers must have something else, information you don't know about. They'll twist any confession I make to something else."

The lawyer shook his head and gave Long Yen a crooked smile. "Pieces in play. Like a shell game. And how do you win the shell game? By never hiding the *zhen zhu* under the cup in the first place."

Long Yen sat back in his chair so he wouldn't correct the man's pronunciation, but also to mask his surprise.

Why had this court-appointed lawyer, with his fresh white face free of the pockmarks of malnutrition, mention the *zhen zhu*, the pearl? Did he know something more than he could say, particularly under the merciless recording eye of the council? Had he actually been placed here by the family?

Hiding the pearl, as one might in a shell game, was a long con. Longer than the one Long Yen had been running.

Hope ran cold fingers, colder than the night side of the planet, down Long Yen's back, raising chicken flesh across his shoulders.

"Tell me more," he demanded, leaning forward, aware that he was catching at the stranger's net, as if it might save him.

———

Long Yen slouched in the outer corridor with two other money changers. They were recent immigrants to Da Chuan—Russians—trying to carve a niche out for themselves. The family tolerated them in their half of the station for reasons only known to them. Long Yen thought they belonged in the other half, with everyone who wasn't Chinese. Let them make a living there.

They stood close enough to the airlocks that the filters couldn't completely clean the air of dust, so a thin red haze filled the enclosed space, muting the sharp lines of boxes and pipes that ran along the ceiling and up and down the curved tunnel walls.

The sound of the blowers was louder here. The sifters

from the surface, who sometimes came inside for trade, liked it that way. They called the sound the blowers made *niao ge*, canary song: If it ever died, they knew to flee.

Long Yen had been practicing his lifts all month. Nei Nei had nearly scalded his fingers with boiling water when she'd seen how sloppy he'd gotten. She'd made his start with family first, his cousin, that stupid ox, Xin Chao. They'd practiced in the tiny kitchen, bumping shoulders, slipping hands in and out of pockets, grabbing IDs and cash.

Once Long Yen had fingers like a snake again, Nei Nei sent him back out to the corridors, first practicing on miners at shift end, when they were slow and not perceptive. Long Yen had to steel himself to stand and watch, his heart pounding. Not because he was afraid of being caught, no. But because watching them made him realize that without the family, he might have turned into a living ghost like them.

Then she sent him after council kids, who Long Yen could have been in school with, preparing for the final exams. He gladly took their trinkets and toys, keeping one of the fancier chronometers for himself, that showed planetary time plus the long count of when the next supply ship would arrive. The station was self-sufficient, and had been from the start, but the planet couldn't support a large enough population to justify factories to create luxury goods.

Finally, Nei Nei declared Long Yen ready. He only knew his target by the red and white scarf she wore to hold back her hair. All the miners wore the same dull gray jumpsuit, which Xin Chao swore were modeled after prison clothes. The only way to tell one from the other sometimes was by the name bling they wore.

Long Yen worked with the money changes for a week, not even looking for his target until two day before, when he'd seen her heading for the mines. Her shift would end now, and Long Yen planned to get close enough to her. Once his job was finished, he'd still have to work as a changer for another week.

It was part of the family's constant teachings. Never make any sudden appearances or disappearances: The goal was to blend and flow, and not be remembered.

As the workers started shuffling out of the mine, Long Yen pushed himself up with a suffering sigh, hiding his true excitement. He held his hand out, first finger extended, then started making circular motions with his hand, indicating his trade: changing The Company script for hard cash that was good anywhere in the station, not just The Company store.

First the men came out, row upon row of sleep walkers, swelling the corridor with their ranks. Long Yen never met the eyes of any of them, never tried to see if a man's soul still remained. He knew they couldn't steal his own life from him like a hungry ghost, but the fear remained. The only sound was the blowers and their soft footsteps through the red dust. None of the men talked or laughed.

Long Yen knew the women were coming because at least a few of them still gossiped together. He thought he spotted his mark as he concluded his business with the last man, her bright red and white bandana bobbing in a sea of yellow, purple, orange, and pink.

Why was she special? Why did Nei Nei insist on her ID? And why here and now?

Long Yen marked her progress, cursing his luck. She

was mid-tide in the sea of miners. How could he reach her?

It looked as though he'd be stuck here for two more weeks.

Suddenly, the money changer in front of Long Yen shouted and shoved the miner he was doing business with away, shouting, "Thief! He steals my money!"

The man fell straight against the girl.

It couldn't be luck. It had to be family.

Didn't Nei Nei trust Long Yen to do the job?

The supposed thief flailed his arms, as if trying to regain his balance.

A bright red line appeared on the cheek of the girl.

Long Yen hurried to her assistance. "Let go!" he yelled, pulling the girl free, rushing her along, plucking her ID easily from her pocket.

"I'm fine, I'm fine, thank you," the girl insisted.

Long Yen nodded and let her go, turning away before she got a good look at him.

She tugged him back around before he could make his escape. "You're not hurt?" she asked.

Long Yen glanced at her face, then away again, quickly. "No, no, I'm fine," he assured her.

He couldn't afford to see her wide brown eyes, or her face as round as a portal window.

"I need to help my friend," he said, bowing and keeping his head turned away. "Excuse me."

Long Yen melted into the crowd as quickly as he could, sliding into the next corridor before the police arrived, the white mice with their nasty biting teeth, dragging him into the council rooms.

He passed the ID over to Nei Nei without looking at it, not questioning, not this time.

He still couldn't help but see the miner again, when her face was plastered all over the screens at the Temple Bar. She was being presented as one of the brightest of the new batch of students who'd passed the civic exams and were moving into government positions.

Or at least someone clean, and well-fed, who happened to look exactly like the miner, who also bore a striking resemblance to one of Long Yen's older cousins.

The worker's card and blood must have been clean, and a close enough match, so the cousin could pass, and the family could gain a new stronghold.

Long Yen raised his glass in a silent toast, though he would have unseen her if he could.

Too much knowledge, particularly for a dragon's son, was never a good thing.

The lawyer still sat. His recording stick, a dull white bar about the size of an antique Mah Johng tile, sat in front of him on the table.

Long Yen paced around the tiny interrogation room as he talked. He knew it didn't matter: the stick picked up every gesture, every nuance, as well as his heart beat, flush rate, and other tells Long Yen couldn't control or train against.

The air regulator still hummed in the background, totally inadequate to draw out the heat and humidity two men generated. Even the dark red clay walls were beginning to sweat.

"So you had access to all government communications," the lawyer said (Chris, maybe?) "And you had an agent in the council."

"Civil service," Long Yen corrected.

"Would you recognize her again?"

Long Yen shrugged. "Maybe. Maybe not. Depends on how important she is. If it was important enough to keep her hidden, she'd have a new face by now. Subtle changes —shifts up or down her cheek bones, flattening or sharpening her nose." She wouldn't have a moon face anymore.

"All right. Anything—"

A loud bang exploded just outside the room, ending with a sharp sizzling sound.

Long Yen froze. The family wouldn't rescue him. He wasn't important enough. They might kill him, but not like this, not big and flashy.

Maybe something had gone wrong in one of the tunnels?

Xin Chao, Long Yen's cousin, threw the door open. Before the lawyer could rise from his chair, Xin Chao shot him with a sizzler, the black net spreading over his chest, burning into his face.

Long Yen grabbed the recording stick from the table and snapped it in two.

There was an official recording, of course. But the family also had access. They must. How else could they have found what room he'd been hidden in?

"Come on!" Xin Chao said, sticking his head back out the door, his sizzler at the ready.

"Where are we going?" Long Yen asked, following close behind though he wanted to keep his distance. Xin Chao wore all black, like some crazy ninja from the screens. Just a brief glance had told Long Yen too much: how small Xin Chao's pupils were, how little he sweated, how unsteady he was on his feet.

It was no safer with this great ox than on his own.

Only two guards lay in the hall. Long Yen felt something between pleased and insulted—on the one hand, only two men had been scoured, but had he only rated two guards? He'd have thought there would have been more.

"Nei Nei's gotten worse," was all Xin Chao said.

That hurried Long Yen along. "Then the last treatments—"

He stopped at Xin Chao's headshake.

"So don't you upset her," Xin Chao said sternly, pulling Long Yen up close, breathing hot, stinking breath in his face.

"I won't," Long Yen said easily. He would have promised the crazy man anything.

"You'll do what she says?"

"Of course," Long Yen assured him.

He didn't know what price Nei Nei expected for his rescue, but he knew it would be high.

He was willing to pay it.

Xin Chao grunted and shoved Long Yen into a tiny utility closet. Thin plastic shelves ran along one rough dirt wall, covered with rusted pipes. Dials and readouts blinked steadily on the other.

Nei Nei crouched like an overgrown basket of rags at the far end. Clear tubes hooked into her nose and fed her air laced with illegal opiates. Thin wires ran from the iron collar around her neck, snaking up to her temples and down under her white cotton blouse. They kept the seizures to a minimum, though she still twitched every few minutes.

But her brown eyes were still dark and clear, and she grasped Long Yen's hand firmly with hers.

"*Xiao zi*," she whispered. "My boy."

Long Yen crouched beside her. "What do you want me to do?"

The muffled sounds of containment doors clanging shut sounded around them.

"There's so much you don't know. So much left to teach you."

Nei Nei twitched hard, then she brought her other hand up to his cheek.

He kissed her overly warm palm. "You have time to teach me," he told her, keeping his voice steady, his tears locked away.

"There's only one thing to tell you," she said with a sad smile.

The closet walls shook. Dirt scrabbled loose and trickled down to the floor.

Fear gripped Long Yen's heart harder than Nei Nei's firm hand.

"*You* were the pearl, my son."

"What? I don't understand—"

"Now, promise me," she said, holding his wrist tight enough that he wondered if there would be bruises. "In *cunwang*, you always choose life. Not death. You hear me? You must choose life for yourself. Live beyond all of us. You were always hidden away. Like the pearl. You must come out of the clouds now."

She jerked his hand toward herself suddenly, slapping it against her flabby belly.

The hard press of the haft of a blade scoured Long Yen's palm.

He jumped away, pressing his back against the rough wall.

Nei Nei slumped in her chair, her blood blossoming across her stomach like the fire of a supply ship at takeoff.

"What have you done?" Xin Chao said as he came rushing in. He bent over, looking more closely at Nei Nei's wound.

A winking light in the corridor caught Long Yen's attention, but he didn't turn toward it.

He couldn't, not yet. Not until he'd done his duty. What he'd promised to Nei Nei.

Reaching his long arms out, Long Yen snagged a pipe from the other wall, and brought it down hard on Xin Chao's unprotected head.

Long Yen then held up his hands and dropped to his knees as the soldier approached, his gun winking still.

A taped confession of the family's doing would never have been enough for the loophole the lawyer had found between the *qing lü* and the colony code.

Not enough to show true contrition for his crimes.

Only by decisively turning against the family could that loophole be exploited.

Only now could Long Yen beg for forgiveness from The Company, and be truly freed.

Long Yen stood and stretched up, his face a moon blossom, always facing the portal that showed the stars.

Up and up they went, this strange new crew buzzing around him. Since it was his first time out of orbit, they let him wander from one port hole to the next, drinking in the sweet cold nectar of the night.

As gravity loosened its hold and Long Yen began to

float, he tethered himself to the hole, the stars blazing like tiny pearls.

The cool metal edges of the ship's walls trembled under his hands as the thrusters engaged and the ship turned.

For the first and last time, Long Yen saw Da Chuan. It hung like a frozen red marble in the sky, shrinking away until it, too, was just a dot of light.

One of many, all loosely connected by the string of humanity.

Finally, Long Yen turned away, turned toward the enormity of his task, the one Nei Nei had set for him.

It had been easy to accept his banishment, to know he'd never return to Da Chuan. The family had been prepared for this, and had a secret receiver ready to be implanted just underneath the new dragon tattoo that itched on his bicep.

The pearl had never been in the game, at least, not the little local game.

No, the family had always wanted a bigger game, with more shells, more cash.

More planets.

And as a true dragon's son, what could Long Yen do but blend and flow, move out and beyond, free to fly among the clouds at last.

AUTHOR'S NOTES

Yet again, another workshop story! I wrote this story for the same workshop that I wrote *The Curious Case of Rabbit and the Temple Goddess*. We were supposed to take our original story and set it many years in the future.

I had tried to write something set in modern day, but I couldn't get any good ideas. When I set it much further out, onto a different planet, I finally started getting somewhere.

If you look closely, you'll see that this story has some of the same characters as the first Rabbit story does. I've written more than one story in this universe, and more of the Rabbit characters show up as well.

TOUCH

He touched me.

Hell.

Why did he do that?

Did he contaminate me? Am I infected now?

Why did he touch me?

Did anyone see him touch me? Where are the cameras?

Don't be obvious, just glance.

There's only one. Over there. Up on the subway platform. To the right.

He touched my left arm. Maybe they didn't see.

The ghost of the contact haunted me, raising the hairs along my neck.

I don't think anyone saw him break protocol. It wasn't like he touched my skin, but my sleeve.

His hands looked bare. Was he wearing noblos, or some other see-thru complex-blocking gloves?

Maybe his hands were *actually* bare. Like some kind of pervert.

No one exposed any skin. Not ever. I'd never be able to wear a short skirt in public. Let alone a sleeveless blouse.

I should burn this jacket, just in case. Put it into the biohazard incineration chute back at the apartment.

That idiot *touched* me. Who knows what contaminants he might have been harboring?

Why did he touch me?

It was deliberate. I know it was.

I couldn't believe the contact when I felt it. I had to look.

He's got on the same wide-spectrum isolation mask I do—mid-range price but high protection, with no incidents of contagion found on the public web. I can't afford to search the private networks beyond those.

His eyes above the gray mask looked kind, not crazed or infected.

However, the photos of John Johnson, the terrorist who released the Singular plague, had friendly eyes. Lonely eyes. He'd merely wanted to find his soulmate, or manufacture one. The ultimate love potion, making both parties instantly attracted to one another, instantly desirable to each other.

He hadn't counted on the mutations. On the writhing masses screwing themselves to death on the streets of the busier cities—Hong Kong, New York, London. The virus spread, and the sight of a man trying to screw a building or a woman impaling herself on a tree became common.

No one touches now, not skin on skin. There are a few who are naturally immune, not that anyone gets themselves tested: Who risks finding out they're biologically incapable of falling in love? That it isn't possible for them to be fully attracted to another?

Of course, there are always rumors that the governments of the world found a cure long ago that they're not sharing, that scared people are easier to manage, while they get rich on barrier technology.

I think the rumors are wrong. Cities are no longer full, and a widely dispersed population is more difficult to manage.

So why did he touch me? Was he, too, looking for his soulmate? Had he watched too many old movies, or even the new city porn, created from video of long-ago security camera, showing strangers casually bumping into each other in the street?

He didn't have permission to touch me. That alone

should have stopped him. Did he get an illicit thrill by breaking the code?

I want to kill him.

His touch stripped me bare again of the illusion that I was safe.

We all pretend we are, the rich secure behind biotech fabrics, the not-so-rich underneath multiple layers of clothing, like wearing our old lives, carrying past into present. The poor just filled their jackets with plastic bags and mattress stuffing.

Was that why he touched me? To remind me of how thin the veneer of safety, of sanity, really is?

I wish I had screamed. I wish I had denounced him for what he is. Even if the police hadn't believed me but only his lies if he'd denied it. Even if it would have meant an isolation ward for the rest of my life, or at least as long as I could afford one, before being passed into a public ward, becoming one of the writhing corridors of flesh.

Maybe he hadn't meant to scare me, but to remind me to see the people around me, not merely as obstacles to avoid, but as companions on this difficult journey. Maybe he wanted me to touch him, too.

He'll never get his wish.

I must go cleanse myself now.

AUTHOR'S NOTES

I had an unpleasant incidence once when I was traveling, with a man reaching over a railing and casually grabbing me. It really pissed me off. I wrote this story in response. I've been told it's very powerful.

ABOUT THE AUTHOR

Leah Cutter writes page-turning fiction in exotic locations, such as a magical New Orleans, the ancient Orient, Hungary, the Oregon coast, rural Kentucky, Seattle, Minneapolis, and many others.

She writes literary, fantasy, mystery, science fiction, and horror fiction. Her short fiction has been published in magazines like *Alfred Hitchcock's Mystery Magazine* and *Talebones*, anthologies like Fiction River, and on the web. Her long fiction has been published both by New York publishers as well as small presses.

Find Leah's books on Knotted Road Press at (www.KnottedRoadPress.com)

Follow her blog at www.LeahCutter.com.

Reviews

It's true. Reviews help me sell more books. If you've enjoyed this story, please consider leaving a review of it on your favorite site.

Come someplace new...

Are you a traveler? Do you enjoy exploring strange new worlds, new cultures, new people?

Journey into the various lands envisioned by Leah Cutter.

Sign up for my newsletter and I'll start you on your travels with a free copy of my book, *The Island Sampler*.

I will never spam you or use your email for nefarious purposes. You can also unsubscribe at any time.

http://www.LeahCutter.com/newsletter/

ABOUT KNOTTED ROAD PRESS

Knotted Road Press fiction specializes in dynamic writing set in mysterious, exotic locations.

Knotted Road Press non-fiction publishes autobiographies, business books, cookbooks, and how-to books with unique voices.

Knotted Road Press creates DRM-free ebooks as well as high-quality print books for readers around the world.

With authors in a variety of genres including literary, poetry, mystery, fantasy, and science fiction, Knotted Road Press has something for everyone.

Knotted Road Press
www.KnottedRoadPress.com

www.ingramcontent.com/pod-product-compliance
Lightning Source LLC
Chambersburg PA
CBHW070530100726
47907CB00004B/1053